For

Luka, Yasmin
&
The Fox Boys

George.
The World's First
Baking Magician

E J YARDLEY

PERFECT PUDDLE PRESS

3

www.perfectpuddlepress.com

PROLOGUE

Pickled Daniels was miserable, tired and drained. Rising in the dead of night had given her a headache. Dressing had been an immense effort. Gathering the energy required to leave her bungalow into the middle of a thunderstorm had almost finished her off. Now here she was balancing on the school roof in the pouring rain, a pathetic, wretched figure. The blackness around her was penetrating. The wind howled as she desperately pulled her tool bag to the ledge, now at the very highest point of St Hindred's School roof.

Holding a mini torch in her mouth, she looked like a grubby, geriatric burglar as she went about her horrid business, grappling with the wires around her feet. Above her, standing proudly to attention, was the gigantic school mast, a satellite dish and aerial rocking in the wind.

"I'll soon have you sorted me darling," she muttered, looking up at the post towering above her.

Then she was up. With no thought for her own safety, she clung desperately onto the pole, hauling her body up the mast. The rain beat down on her face. It was no place for an elderly lady to be but she had work to do.

Finally, she hung at the topmost edge of the beam, stabilising her weight on the slippery tip of the mast. Gently she reached into her grizzly bag of tools and grasped a hammer. Carefully prising it out, her hands started to ache. This was important, it had to be done. The wind swirled up, snatching it out of her grip. It plunged to the ground.

"Noooooooooo.........," she screamed into the darkness, "...no, no, no, no, no. No matter. I have other nice surprises in me bag. Something much bigger and better than you, you horrible hammer. Where are you me sweetheart...". She smiled to herself.

Delicately she teased out another ghastly implement, revealing a large gold crowbar. She raised the tool high into the air and brought it down in one swift movement. It made contact with the metal, creating an almighty crack. The huge pole shuddered and wobbled in the wind then slowly began to tilt - then tumble at speed, finally snapping in half. Pickled Daniels shielded her face as the other end flew towards her. The metal descended, and with a tremendous crash, the post came to a halt. Then silence, slowly the pitter patter of the rain returned as Pickled Daniel's hearing recovered.

She cautiously opened an eye, a big grin forming on her face. Sliding down she started to hum a show tune. This was going to be a great day. A really, really, really, really great day.

MEET THE TEAM

George

Marley

Sam

1 GEORGE & MARLEY

George opened his curtains wide and looked out at the bright sunlight on the garden. The storm had passed during the night. The world appeared as if painted brand new. Dressing as quick as he could, he peeled his screwed-up school clothes from the floor.

George's room was tiny. He'd helped decorate it in his own style. Posters of football stars lined up next to famous magicians. His particular favourite was a street magician standing in New York in front of a giant skyscraper, his arms held out, as if ready to make it disappear. George surveyed his posters, pulling on his clothes in a hurry. Clutching his football, he raced downstairs.

Tuesday meant after school baking club, and George loved it. Bouncing into the kitchen, he kicked the ball in front of him.

"Morning, George," said dad not moving from his newspaper. "What have I said about playing football in the kitchen. Come on, put it away or you'll be late for school. So, what's the plan for today then?"

"Oh, it's not good news. Mrs Tinsley's saying that the whole school has to watch that silly Royal Wedding," said George settling down to pour out his cereal, his feet playing with the ball under the table.

"Oh yes, I was just reading about it here. The Queen's second cousin's, dog's, friend's, milkman's daughter or something." George's dad fluffed the newspaper out to show him the article.

"Yes." George sighed. "Mrs Tinsley's already got loads of plates and cups with their faces on them all over her office. She loves the royal family."

George's dad looked at his watch.

"Oh goodness, I'm going to be late." He rose from the table in a panic patting his trousers.

"Has anyone seen my wallet?" he screamed up the hall at no-one in particular, racing around like a befuddled ticket inspector. There was a loud knock on the front door.

"It's Marley," shouted mother from upstairs. "Time to go."

George's school was just over a mile from his house, every day his best friend Marley walked to school with him.

"OK," shouted George, scrabbling to put a final scoop of cereal into his mouth.

"Wait for Phoebe," his mother screamed from upstairs.

George huffed. The last thing an eleven-year-old boy wants is to have his little sister with him on the way to school, even if she is only two years younger, it's SOOOOOOOOOOOOO annoying. Phoebe trotted down the stairs, her hair in bunches with a bright purple flower on a clip.

"I'm not walking to school with you with that," said George pointing at the purple lump in her hair.

"Why not?" said Phoebe, "I look very pretty." She walked straight past George, opening the front door.

"Hello, Marley."

"Hi Phoebe," said Marley. "What's that?" He pointed at Phoebe's hair. "It looks like a purple bogey."

Phoebe scrunched her face up, going red in the process. "It is not a bogey, Marley. It is a handmade flower clip that I made with my mum. So there." She poked her tongue out, crossing her arms in defiance.

George pushed her back, "Come on Marley, let's go - Phoebe's not ready, she'll have to walk by herself." He bundled Marley out of the door down the front path.

"I am ready," said Pheobe, grabbing her school bag. "Byyyyeeeeeee mum," she shouted as the door shut behind her. And so it was that on that particular Tuesday George walked to school with his little sister who had a purple flower in her hair that looked somewhat like a crusty bogey.

George and Phoebe's school was old, bleak and slightly ramshackled – it could have done with a lick of paint. It always had a faint pong of disinfectant where Pickled Daniels the school cleaner had been a little too heavy on the bleach the previous night. George wondered if Pickled Daniels was very well; whenever George saw her, she seemed to have difficulty standing up, let alone clean. Of course, Pickled Daniels wasn't her real name, it was Mrs Daniels, but George had even heard some of the teachers' call her Pickled Daniels when they thought no one was listening, he assumed it was because she liked to eat pickles.

When George, Phoebe and Marley arrived at the school gates, Pickled Daniels was there munching on an apple. She was a wiry, altogether ugly woman whose hair grew at odd, obtuse angles from the top of her prickly head. She cherished wearing her cleaning overalls until they wore out, they hadn't seen the inside of a washing machine for years. As they got close, she gave an almighty sneeze sending out chunks of apple and spit all over them.

"Oh...sorry," she muttered sarcastically, eyeing them with disgust, a dim outline of a smile on her face. She swigged from a bottle she held in a brown paper bag. Marley smelt the faint odour of stale vinegar mixed with a sweaty flip-flop, he wrinkled his nose.

"Mrs Daniels, it must be really thirsty work being a school cleaner. You're always drinking from that bottle you keep in that bag," said Phoebe brightly.

"Yep. That's right kid," replied Pickled Daniels smirking. "It's very thirsty work all the stuff I do. Anyway, it's none of your business. Leave me alone."

Taking another gulp, she wobbled from one foot to another. Her hooked nose twitched in the sunlight.

George wasn't sure how old Pickled Daniels was, he guessed at one hundred and thirty-five. Flinging her apple core onto the road, she shuffled into school. Phoebe's face crumpled.

"Phoebe, I don't think you should talk to her," said George. "She's horrible, smelly and nasty. Mum said she's been working at the school forever. No one likes her."

"Well I do," stated Phoebe turning on her heels, her nose held high.

George sighed.

2 THE GORGEOUS PICKLED DANIELS

Now it's a known fact that if you work in a school as a teacher, you must tolerate children. It's essential, without this skill you can't teach. It's not easy trying to persuade a bunch of screaming nine-year-olds to understand the basics of maths if you don't adore kids.

Think of your own teacher; I imagine they are a pretty nice person - they probably say lovely, kind things to you. Teachers walk into schools all over the country each day with their heads held high telling themselves - *I love my career, nothing gives me more pleasure than sitting down in front of a brainy bunch of children and teaching them everything I know.*

The more they do it, the more pleasure it gives and so by the time they are close to retirement they have a deep loving relationship with their careers and teaching. They march through life on a high knowing they have the best job in the whole wide world.

Now, if you're the school cleaner, you don't necessarily have the same high ideals regarding children or indeed the same profound love of your work. Pickled Daniels was one such person. Not only did she have a deep hatred for her job, her career, and her life, above all this she had a profound loathing of happiness. And the happiest people she knew were children.

They were all so smiley, giggly and enthusiastic about life. Horrible children. She had a natural inclination to despise them all. Pickled Daniels did not recall feeling very contented when she was a child, so she couldn't really understand why they were always so happy, **it made her mad**! You see she was so mean, so nasty, so spiteful, so vindictive and ever so vile that she took enormous joy from seeing children upset. A little tear or the screwed up face of a five-year-old was pure pleasure for her. Pickled Daniels did everything she could to spoil fun and frivolity wherever she went. You might think it odd then that she chose to work at a school, but it wasn't strange to her, it merely meant she was in the best place possible to upset them.

Pickled Daniels lived next to the school. Thirty years ago her little bungalow would have been part of it. In those times the caretaker lived on site and spent most of their time cleaning, fixing and maintaining the school and its grounds, as well as locking and unlocking the many doors at the beginning and end of the school day.

Now her bungalow was separate having been sold off by the council many years ago, though she still felt like it was part of it. She could spy the school from her kitchen window (or could if she wiped it hard enough to remove the grime).

Pickled Daniels spent most of her evenings not cleaning, or fixing, or being helpful - which is what you'd expect from the dedicated school cleaner. No, she spent most nights *destroying children's school work*. This was the beauty of having access to the school after hours when no one was around.

It gave her enormous amounts of pleasure to see a seven-year-old child standing with a broken doll knowing she'd pulled its arm off the night before, she was utterly despicable. She loved to rip pages from exercise books, daub paint on the year two art, slightly amend a small boy's coursework, change scores in a test, disrupt a science experiment. But she was devious. She always made sure that the changes she made were tiny, little by little, small steps which just made some of the children look like they'd messed up, not a lot, no serious errors, only the odd thing here and there.

If a science experiment went wrong, the teachers just said they must have a made a mistake in setting it up, or if all the class got one question wrong in a test, no one would notice. Oh, but it gave Pickled Daniels such a feeling of warmth. If she messed something up one evening, she would make a point of hanging around the door of the classroom the next morning. She'd pretended to clean a door handle or sweep the floor just so she could listen in and hear the consequences of her actions. "Nathan. Why did you forget to answer that last question in the maths test?", or "Ellis, why didn't you water the seeds? They've all died", or "Joseph. There's a page missing in your homework book". Pickled Daniels would go walking down the corridor with a smile on her face. So you see, she really was a very horrid woman.

Today she was busy in her bungalow preparing for her night's work. For many years she had been keeping a journal detailing the individual ideas and plans she had thought up for terrorising children. Having had fifty years experience in spoiling children's fun, there wasn't much Pickled Daniels didn't know about stopping laughter and enjoyment. All of it was documented in her ghastly *Compendium*, or to give it it's full title

The Master Compendium of De-Funning

which was scrawled across the front in big, brown letters in Pickled Daniels own scratchy handwriting. Pickled Daniels had a habit of speaking to the *Compendium* as if it were a person. It was the only thing she really loved.

"Come down and see me, my beautiful girl," croaked Pickled Daniels stretching up to the top shelf. The book was old, hefty and enormous. She gave it a quick wipe with her arm.

"Yes, mummy's here," she said, looking at the book with loving eyes. Sitting down she carefully balanced the book on her lap. Reaching for her reading glasses, she took a quick swig from a bottle - the world span a little. Pickled Daniels loved to drink sherry in the afternoon, it made the end of the school day so much more bearable (or rum or port, she wasn't fussy). The *Compendium* was well thumbed with all sorts of horrid things sticking out of it. There were scrawled pencil plans, maps showing traps, doodles, cartoons and all manner of wicked thoughts she'd had. She peered over her specs. The volume was huge.

"Now, where's bit 'bout clubs. Come on darling, show mummy." Flicking the pages, she skimmed each one briefly for a solution.

"Mmmm...spiders in school dinners, no that's not it. Wet wellies traps. No..." Near the end of the book, she eventually found the section she was looking for.

"Very good me darling. Here it is...school clubs and how to stop em...I knew you wouldn't let me down." She bent forward and gave the book a kiss. Her current pet hate was baking club, baking club was a total disaster. It meant the little sprats were at school longer than the school day and she had to start cleaning later than usual. Bending over the side table, she picked up a magnifying glass staring carefully at the horrid text.

"Now then sweetheart...what do we need to do?"

3 EVERYONE LOVES A ROYAL WEDDING

The whole school sat cross-legged in the school field as Mrs Tinsley, the headmistress, tinkered with the TV perched on the grass. It was 'Royal Wedding Day' and Mrs T, as she was affectionately known, was making every effort to get the children involved. George and Marley had desperately tried to sit near the back, but they had somehow found themselves pushed onto the front row. That meant no mucking about, every teachers' eye was on you.

"Now, don't worry children. It won't be long before we can get this old thing working. I believe the wedding is on channel one hundred and sixty-three, isn't it lovely being out in the open air," said Mrs T in her plummy voice, jiggling with the remote control - taking a deep breath to prove the air was fresh. She was dressed head to toe in red, white and blue velvet, finished off with a small union jack brooch. She appeared like a walking, talking flag - but she felt incredibly posh and very British.

None of them were worried. Not one of the children had ever heard of Princess What's-her-face or Prince That's-his-name, a distant relative of the Queen who were due to walk down the aisle. An obscure digital TV channel had promised to show the whole dreadfully long wedding ceremony. But the television revealed a mass of white snow, unable to tune itself.

"Well, this is *not* good enough. Oh dear, oh dear."

Mrs T had resorted to merely stabbing every button on the remote.

"Mr Savage, please find Mrs Daniels immediately, she was the last to put this away. We need to get this sorted pronto." Mr Savage gave a little salute and jogged into the school looking like an ostrich who had just eaten some jelly babies.

The children mumbled as the proceedings stopped. George played with his shoelaces to relieve the boredom until, eventually, Mr Savage returned looking sheepish.

"Where is she? Mr Savage....where is she" demanded Mrs T, a frown forming on her brow.

Pickled Daniels appeared looking even grubbier than usual. Her tunic was covered in stains, and a stench of vegetables emanated from her.

"Ah, there you are Mrs Daniels. Now, we have a problem. I can't get this television to work. I've plugged in the satellite cable extension, but nothing's happening. The children are absolutely desperate to watch the royal wedding."

Pickled Daniels ambled over to the TV set, tutting to herself. She fiddled with the back a bit while the children silently watched, most of them pinching their noses.

"Mmmm...what a shame...satellite's broken I think. Must have been the storm, Mrs Tinsley. I imagine it's that big mast on the school roof. Perhaps it got damaged in the big storm. Oh, how awful for the children. Powerful it were. Saw the news, they said the wind got lots of things. What a terrible, terrible shame for the children. Perhaps they should go home, I wants them all to see it. Go on children, time to go home. Come on off you go..." said Pickled Daniels raising her hands bustling for the children to stand up. The whole speech a master class in acting.

"What twaddle Mrs Daniels. Of course they aren't going home, that would be absolutely ridiculous. This is frightfully unfortunate. I'm very cross about this, we must be able to do something," said Mrs T striding back and forth.

The field was quiet waiting for their great leader to speak. She marched slowly in front of them up and down like a caged tiger at a zoo. Pickled Daniels stood with arms firmly folded looking grumpily at the children. Finally, after what seemed an eternity, she spoke.

"No matter Mrs Daniels," Mrs T sparked up excitedly like she had just cracked the secret of why school dinners always taste of rubber.

"**We can stream it.** That's what everyone does nowadays isn't it." Mrs T wasn't one who kept up with the latest technology. "All we need is, what do they call it…..wi-fi, that's it, wif-fi." Mrs T was hopping about at the front of the field getting very excited.

"You just need to turn on the internet box in my office Mrs Daniels. The connection is slow, but it will be OK for an emergency. **And this is an emergency**. The Queen will be arriving at the church shortly, and I mustn't miss it. Erm.... I mean the children mustn't miss it. **Go and sort it immediately.**"

Pickled Daniels looked like she'd been poked with an extremely long stick. Her mouth open, unable to respond - eyes blinking like a manic pigeon.

"Come on Mrs Daniels," chided Mrs T, "we haven't long."

Pickled Daniels unhurriedly walked off the field, a look of disgust on her face.

Five minutes later Pickled Daniels still hadn't returned. The children were getting restless.

"This is no good, this is no good at all," yelled Mrs T looking at her watch for the hundredth time, now tapping her foot. She surveyed the sea of heads in front of her. "Right...erm. yes....erm....George, Marley - go and find Mrs Daniels will you and hurry her along."

George and Marley grudgingly rose from the throng.

"Do we have to?" whined George. "Can't someone else do it?"

"What's wrong with you George. Someone stole your legs. Go on, go on, go and find her...and hurry.....this is now a major emergency." Mrs T flapped her arms as if that would make them move quicker.

George and Marley slumped from the field. They crept along the corridors in silence, like curious spiders inching along a drainpipe. With everyone else outside it was eerily quiet. They'd never walked alone around the school before.

"Where is she? I don't like this. It's too quiet. Why did we have to find her? You go in front," whispered Marley, pushing George ahead of him.

"That's not fair. You go in front," replied George stepping back and pushing Marley.

"No, you." Marley shoved George.

"No, you."

"No, you."

"OK. I'll do it. I'm not scared," said George finally taking the lead, his heart beating a little faster. They peered into the school reception, but it was empty. They slowly sneaked towards Mrs T's office. Marley scanned the horizon.

"Hello my sweetheart, are you Mrs Tinsley's little friend?" came Pickled Daniels voice from behind them. George and Marley jumped round to face her. She stood in the office cupboard, the flashing internet box in hand, with the door wide open.

"Sorry, were you talking to us?" stammered George.

"What you two wants?" screeched Pickled Daniels.

Marley started trembling and held onto George's sleeve, gulping in air. His hands incredibly clammy.

"No. I certainly wasn't talking to you two cretins. I was talking to my friend here." She held the box aloft.

"M...M…M…M...Mrs Tinsley asked us to fetch you. Everyone's waiting. She's worried we are going to miss the start."

"Well they'll just have to wait, won't they. I couldn't find the box thing, this one's broken."

"No it isn't. You've turned it on. The lights are flashing on the front of it," added Marley.

"Don't argue with me, you idiots. It is

broken." Pickled Daniel sneered.

She glared at them for what seemed an eternity. Marley swallowed and looked down. George's legs had begun to shake, his feet wobbled. Slowly she picked up the box in two grubby hands, raised it above her head and held it high, a grin of triumph on her face; finally, she smashed it down onto a raised knee. There was an almighty crash as it fractured in two.

"Yes. It's definitely broken." Pickled Daniels smiled broadly, a smirk forming.

George and Marley stood like a pair of astonished guppy fish - their mouths wide open.

4 NO ONE LIKES A SOGGY BOTTOM

Later that evening school baking club was in full swing. Mrs Walker had been directing everyone for the last half an hour, desperately trying to sound like a knowledgeable bake-off judge. George and Marley were working hard in the workspace next to the kitchen door.

Marley pushed a bowl towards George.

"Have you heard her?" whispered Marley.

"Heard who?" said George not looking up from his weighing scales.

"Pickled Daniels of course. Who else do you think? She's been scratching around the whole time behind that door. That's why I wanted to swap places with you earlier."

"Don't be silly. I haven't heard anything," said George.

Mrs Walker stepped to the front of the class.

"I hope none of you has a *soggy bottom* and that you're all being *star bakers*," said Mrs Walker, beaming. The class gave a collective groan.

There's nothing worse than a teacher trying to be funny thought George.

A loud sigh came from behind the door, and the whole class looked over. The door was closed, but it sounded like someone was right there, camping out next to the entrance. Mrs Walker slowly tiptoed over to the door and pushed her ear up against it. The class held their breath. In one swift movement, she yanked the door open. Pickled Daniels tumbled into the room like a clumsy clown, landing in a messy heap. Some of the class gasped, while others giggled. She sat motionless like a beached seal.

"What on earth are you doing Mrs Daniels?" said Mrs Walker surveying Pickled Daniels flopped out on the floor. Pickled Daniels gathered herself up, brushing down her clothes.

"Oh, Mrs Walker. So sorry Mrs Walker, I do apologise - I was like walking past, and I notices some marks on this here door. I was examining them to see what polish I might need you see - you see tomorrow I'm cleanin' em - you opened the door, and I sorts of fell in here. Honestly."

Pickled Daniels gradually scanned the room, a look of disgust on her face. She gave her best "puppy dog" eyes to Mrs Walker. The class remained silent and very tense.

Mrs Walker stared at Pickled Daniels unable to think of a reasonable response. Pickled Daniels glared back, breathing heavily, a small ball of mucus gathering on the end of her nose. Marley nudged George.

"See. She was listening at the door," he whispered to George. "I'm sure of it. I thought there was an odd smell over that side of the room. She's been there for ages. She's been following us from lesson to lesson since this morning."

George didn't want to reply, he didn't want to bring attention to himself in front of Pickled

Daniels again. He was **terrified** of her but didn't want to admit it to Marley. Of course, if he'd discussed it with Marley he would know that he was also **really** nervous of Pickled Daniels and didn't want to admit it to George either. He tried to nod as subtly as possible.

"Thank you, Mrs Daniels," said Mrs Walker. "We must carry on, the children's parents will be here to pick them up shortly."

Pickled Daniels gathered her things up and shuffled out of the room murmuring, "So sorry, so sorry."

Marley caught her eye, freaking out he snapped his gaze to the window.

Mrs Walker turned to the class, a little ruffled. "OK. We have five minutes left. We need to tidy up."

Picking up a cloth George explained to Marley about a magic illusion he'd seen on YouTube at the weekend and how he would really like to learn magic.

"Well, you could learn a trick if you wanted to, what's stopping you. There are loads of websites about magic you could look at," said Marley. George thought about it while he did the washing up. Yes, perhaps he could learn a trick or two and become like one of the street magicians he admired. He thought a little more. While Marley stacked the bowls back into the cupboard, George had a brainwave. He nipped to the other side of the work surface and grabbed three of his rock cakes, lined them up and covered them with a towel. Marley focused on George stood behind the worktop.

"What are you doing?"

"Magic," said George.

"What? You haven't got time. Mrs Walker wants us out of here in two minutes, and your mum will be here to pick us up. When I said you could learn a trick, I didn't mean right now." Marley nervously glanced around the kitchen. Everyone was packing up.

"Well, I'll be quick," said George smirking. "Stand there and watch." George didn't really know what he was doing but started to improvise his first big magic trick.

"OK - you see before you three, very well baked, rock cakes." George carried on as if he was a seasoned street magician. Marley's friend Yasmin turned around to watch as well. George's growing audience spurred him on.

"Right - you can see they are in position here." He picked up the tea towel to show them with a flourish. "I will now place this tea towel back over the three of them."

With his right hand, George used a quick sleight of hand to pull one of the cakes to the edge of the table. Flicking the cake, it fell on top of his right shoe. With his right hand, he formed a lump in the towel where the rock cake had been.

"So you see," he continued, "three cakes."

To his amazement Marley and Yasmin hadn't noticed, nodding in agreement that the three cakes were under the towel. George ploughed on with his presentation, though he now had a cake balanced on his foot which made the whole process a little more difficult.

"I would now like you to take this magic...erm...magic..." George picked up the only thing to hand, "fork. Yes, take this magic fork and wave it over the towel whispering the magic words...erm...the magic words..."

"Yer," said Marley, "what are the magic words?"

George wasn't prepared, he looked around the room, and his eye caught a sign above the door.

"Erm...the magic words are...yes, the magic words are...Fire...Exit."

Marley grabbed the fork, waving it over the

towel, then in unison with Yasmin said, "Fire Exit," both of them grinning wildly.

George's foot, balancing the cake, was beginning to strain. He whipped back the towel and gestured to show one had disappeared. Spinning around he flicked the cake from his foot into the air and caught it in one hand; he knew his Saturdays playing football would be useful one day. Geroge rammed the cake into his mouth as Marley and Yasmin clapped and cheered. George couldn't turn now, he had a cake stuffed in his cheeks like a fat squirrel, which he was desperately trying to munch on.

"What's going on over here?" queried Mrs Walker returning to their table. "What's all this mess? You should be tidied up by now."

Marley and Yasmin froze, George had his back to Mrs Walker struggling to swallow the mass of cake.

"George?" said Mrs Walker. "George, turn round and tell me why you haven't tidied this up, some of the parents are here now."

George looked at the floor, a blush appearing on his cheeks with shame.

"Sorry Mrs Walker," he mumbled, spraying cake crumbs everywhere, covering the floor.

Marley and Yasmin burst out laughing.

5 WHO DOESN'T LOVE SHOWBIZ?

The next day George and Marley were on their way to school. Marley had kicked a small stone all along the street, and he still had control of it. He was very impressed with his football skills. George had other things on his mind.

"Do you think Pickled Daniels had been behind that door for the whole of baking club?" George asked, twirling his bag around his body.

"I reckon," replied Marley, still concentrating on kicking his small stone. He sent it flying to the other side of the pavement.

"There was a nasty smell over that side for a good twenty minutes before she fell into the kitchen. That was funny though wasn't it?" Marley chuckled to himself.

"Yer, it was, but she really scares me. I try not to look at her in case she puts a curse on me or something. Jake in year five told me she has some freaky, evil powers. He told me to not look her in the eye, or I'd have bad luck all year," said George.

"My dad said she should have retired years ago and he doesn't know why they let her carry on, she must be over one hundred years old by now. And why did she break that internet box as well? Mrs T was so angry when she realised she couldn't watch that silly royal wedding." Marley gave the stone another nonchalant kick.

"I don't know. I'm starting to think she does a lot of the bad things which happen in the school. Well, anyway. Don't make eye contact with her. I'm serious," said George sternly.

"OK, OK. No problem."

They carried on walking in silence.

It was time for school assembly. Every Wednesday the classes were crammed into the main hall to sing various hymns and hear tedious announcements. George and Marley thought it was the most boring part of the whole week. Phoebe on the other hand quite enjoyed it as sometimes Mrs T gave out prizes or announced the winners from school competitions. So every week there was an outside chance she might actually win something.

This week it was definitely, officially, utterly monotonous for everyone. There wasn't any singing and Mrs Jarvey, the year five teacher, had just given a long talk about the forthcoming (very, very, very, very, very tedious) stuffy museum field trip, something which George, Marley and Phoebe wouldn't be involved in.

Finally, it was Mrs T's turn to address the pupils. As she rose from her seat, the slight mumblings which had begun after Mrs Jarvey's talk stopped immediately. Every child in the whole school behaved in front of Mrs Tinsley, who wouldn't? She was incredibly strict. She stood in front of the school like a confident cockerel.

"Very good children," started Mrs T. "I have a couple of announcements to make. Firstly non-uniform day will be two weeks today. Please remember to bring in your two-pound donation and wear clothes of your favourite colour. Secondly, remember it is Judo grading on Thursday - please remember to bring in your grading books, especially you Marley and Michael." Marley turned a deep crimson, George mimed a laugh.

Mrs Tinsley continued, "Punctuality. I have said it before, and I will repeat it again. Please make sure you are here by eight forty-five at the latest. I will be sending out letters to your parents later this week to remind them of this. Now, I would like to hand over to Mrs Walker who has an announcement."

"Thank you, Mrs Tinsley," said Mrs Walker standing. "Now, I have some exciting news for you. The teachers and I have decided that we have a lot of amazing and undiscovered talent in the school, whether it be singing, playing a musical instrument, reading, acting or something else. And no Jake, that does not include a talent for having a whole bag of wotsits in your mouth at the same time." There was some giggling at the back of the assembly hall. "So we have decided that we should host a talent show. I've spoken to all the teachers, and they are all thrilled by the prospect. It's about having fun and showcasing your particular skill, as well as raising some much-needed funds for the parent and teachers association. Parents will be invited, and we hope to see you all perform something extra special."

Mrs T rose from her chair again smiling broadly at the crowd.

"And children. While I don't encourage such habits, we have kindly been given a prize by one of the parents who works at the local sweet factory. The winner of the talent show will receive a year's supply of pick and mix sweets." Mrs T began applauding, her broad smile nearly hitting her ears. The school hall erupted in noise.

Pickled Daniels had been perched at the back of the hall during Mrs Walker's announcement and heard it all. Now she was traipsing back to her bungalow across the school playground thinking about the show and what it meant. Kids staying late after school practising their instruments, preparing the school hall for the show, cleaning it afterwards and loads more work.

There was a mad shriek from behind her. "Mrs Daniels...Mrs Daniels." Mrs Tinsley was running like a demented duchess across the playground towards her. Picked Daniels sighed.

"Mrs Daniels," said Mrs T puffing as she caught up with her, "I've been meaning to talk to you. I'd hoped to tell you about this talent show before you heard it in the assembly as it will mean a little more work for you in the coming few weeks."

"I knows," murmured Pickled Daniels looking to the floor and kicking some invisible dirt with her foot.

"Yes, well I'm sorry you heard like that. There will be quite a few days when children will be here late so you'll need to lock up and so forth, and we will need to discuss plans for the day itself."

"Yer...well I don't like it interrupting my routine, Margaret," Pickled Daniels said slowly, still not looking her in the eye.

"No, I quite understand Mrs Daniels," continued Mrs Tinsley," which also brings me to another delicate matter which I feel we need to discuss shortly Mrs Daniels. I know we've always been willing to carry on employing you past your official retirement age, but I think maybe the job is perhaps stretching you slightly now. Wouldn't you like to retire Mrs Daniels?" Mrs T held Pickled Daniels in a stare. Waiting for a revelation.

"No I would not," replied Pickled Daniels," I love seeing the tiny faces of the children, Margaret. It gives me such pleasure in me old age." *Well, seeing the little idiots cry* thought Pickled Daniels.

Mrs T looked at her thoughtfully, *what a lovely thing for Mrs Daniels to have said*.

"Well. Think about it. We should discuss this in the coming weeks."

Mrs T walked away leaving Pickled Daniels to ponder on all the nasty surprises she had in store for the dear little children.

6 DEAR OLD UNCLE ERNIE

George lived with his mum, dad, sister and his great-uncle Ernie. Ernie had only been living with them for the last eighteen months. He was George's Grandad's brother, though George had never known his Grandad who died long before he was born. Ernie was the only old person George knew.

He'd lived in sheltered accommodation but had to move in with them after the warden found him cooking flowers for tea one night. Flowers don't have enough vitamins in them, so it was decided he needed family to look after him.

Ernie Ferris was eighty-six years old, deaf as a post, and stubborn with it, so he could possibly rank in the top one hundred worst people to live with in the world – and to say he had a wind problem would be an understatement.

The weekend meant football for George, and gymnastics for Phoebe. It was a glorious, hot sunny morning and George rushed down to the kitchen for breakfast while tucking his football shirt into his shorts. Great Uncle Ernie sat at the kitchen table while George's mother cooked scrambled eggs. George could sense that his mother had already had a tough morning with Ernie.

"So what is it you want for breakfast Ernie?" his mother said in a raised voice with her back to the kitchen. George sat down next to Ernie.

"What did I break first? Never broke anything dear," replied Ernie, "not one bone. Though a few years after the war my heart was broken. I suppose that counts as the thing that broke first. I've never really thought about it like that. Why do you ask dear?"

"No Ernie," shouted George's mother turning towards Ernie with a wooden spoon in her hand pointing it at him as if in battle. "Not break first….I said **what would you like for breakfast**?"

"Oh... Porridge dear," replied Ernie, oblivious to his deafness.

"We haven't got porridge, Ernie." George's mother sighed.

"I'll have eggs," said Ernie.

Ernie stared out of the window, deep in his own thoughts.

"All ready for football George?" said Dad entering the kitchen.

"Yer, ready Dad. Hope Marley's not late again - we were put in the rotten team in training last week 'cause we were late," said George.

"I'm sure he'll be on time this week."

George's dad turned to Ernie. "You OK uncle?"

"Yes...fine...fine," Ernie said.

George poured his cereal into the bowl and started thinking about Ernie. He didn't really know anything about him, Ernie had turned up some months ago, moved in and was living in the same house, but George realised he'd hardly talked to Ernie and hadn't really made any effort to get to know him.

"Uncle Ernie?"

"Yes," he replied, looking up.

"What was she like? The girl you were talking about, the one you said had broken your heart. How old were you?" said George inquisitively.

"How cold were we? It wasn't cold - it was summer. Yes, in the summer, I must have been about seventeen or eighteen maybe. I was working for a firm of accountants. Oh, it was a horrible nasty job, but at the time it paid the bills. Agnes was her name, I met her by chance walking along the river bank. I used to walk it every day as a route home, and every day I would pass Agnes walking her dog. We started with a few friendly nods as we passed each other and then one day her dog got loose, wouldn't come back to her and it got caught in some weeds in the river. I heard her screaming and ran to the spot, she was a complete mess. So I simply jumped in and rescued the dog. After that, she fell for me."

"You jumped in?" said George wide-eyed, amazed at his great uncles' heroics.

"No, I didn't bump into anything, I said I jumped in. Goodness, it was cold in there I can tell you."

"So what happened to her then, Ernie?" chimed in George's dad sitting down at the table.

"Don't know," Ernie replied slowly, staring into the middle distance. "We were courting for eighteen months, but I had to do my National Service, joined the army. I went away, and we lost touch. She was lovely that's all I remember."

"Well, plenty more fish in the sea ay Ernie," said George's dad.

"Not really, no," replied Ernie flatly. He carried on eating his breakfast in silence.

Dad gave George a wink.

"What's National Service?" asked George.

"Ah, good question George." Dad took a bite of toast before continuing. "It's exactly what you and Marley need that's what. In the olden days, every young man had to join the army, it was the law."

"Oh," said George. "Can you do magic, baking and play football in the army?"

"No,"

"Well, I wouldn't like it then."

George's mum deposited a large plate of scrambled eggs on the table.

"So George and Phoebe," she said, "what have you decided to do in the school talent show?"

The parents had received a long letter from Mrs Walker praising the talent in the school and prompting parents to get the children involved as much as possible.

"The letter said that me and your Dad can be involved in your act if you want us to be."

"Yes, I used to be a great dancer. Perhaps I could do that with you?" added George's Dad. They both burst out laughing, George's mum nearly choked on her eggs.

George and Phoebe were mortified. What could be worse than your Mum and Dad joining you on stage and dancing!

Ernie chimed in, oblivious to the laughing. "I was a great dancer too." He added.

George stormed out of the room.

"You're not joining in," he shouted as he marched up the stairs.

George slammed his door and lay on his bed daydreaming. He knew exactly what he was going to do, and it certainly didn't involve dancing. George was going to combine the arts of magic and baking. He would be the first baking magician the world has ever seen.

Though thinking about it - it would require some planning!

7 WHO'S SEEN A GIANT SQUIRREL?

Football training took place at the other side of town, and as Phoebe had gymnastics in the hall next to the recreation ground, Dad drove them both every Saturday. They bundled into the car and set off, stopping briefly to pick up Marley who was standing in his driveway with two different coloured socks on, and half his t-shirt tucked in.

"Your socks don't match Marley," said George's dad, chuckling.

"I know," puffed Marley. "I've been running around the house trying to find matching ones. Couldn't though, my mum went crazy and said I'd have to wear these. My Dad then said that my mum hadn't ironed his jeans either. My mum went mad and said that Dad was welcome to move out into a hotel." This made George's dad laugh even more.

"You look silly," said Phoebe.

"Thanks, Phoebe," replied Marley.

When they arrived George and Marley headed to the playing field, and Phoebe ran to the hall. George's dad picked up the newspaper, settled into his seat and gave a big sigh of contentment – this was his only chance for peace each week.

George and Marley were put through their paces at the training session. Mr Rowlands, the football coach, had them line up at the penalty spot and kick the football into an empty goal. They had both missed, and coach Rowlands sent them off to run around the pitch ten times as punishment. They were jogging around the edge of the football pitch for the fifth time when Marley plucked up the courage to ask George about Pickled Daniels again.

"You know Pickled Daniels...?" said Marley.

"Yer," replied George, slightly puffing. "What about her?"

"Well since the royal wedding thing I've been thinking about all the things that go wrong at school."

"What? What do you mean?"

"OK, do you remember when Mrs Walker found three rats in her room last year. Then Pickled Daniels took them away and said they wouldn't be seen again. Then like, a month later, three rats appeared in Mr Savage's room, and Pickled Daniels just happened to be passing when they were running all over the place, then Molly Roberts fainted and was sick over Mr Savage."

"Yes." George sniggered. "But that was just coincidence, and it was quite funny."

"Yer, well what about the time the toilets flooded just as the year twos were going out to break and they all got their feet covered in water sewage, then Mrs Tinsley came in and slipped on that brown muck on the floor. Well, Pickled Daniels was there then as well wasn't she?"

"You mean she slipped on a poo," said George. They both started laughing. George was finding it difficult to jog and giggle at the same time. They heard a shout from Mr Rowlands in the distance, barking for them to go faster.

"But she's the school cleaner so she would have been there," continued George.

"Yes, but what about the vegetable patch apparently being eaten by giant squirrels - which only Pickled Daniels saw, who's ever seen a giant squirrel? And what about the time the popcorn machine went wrong before the fete, and there were millions of pieces of popcorn in the dining room." Marley counted the points on his fingers, his voice rising. "And what about all the violins being out of tune before the school concert when they had only been tuned twenty minutes before, and also the time the school bus had a three punctures so we couldn't go to the pantomime. And we know for a fact she broke that wi-fi box, we saw it."

George stopped running, his hand on his knees to catch his breath. He was silent, his face in a frown.

"You know, you're right. When you think about when anything odd happens, she's always there, hanging about. You can't miss her anyway with the smell. When have we ever had a science experiment go right? Something always goes missing, or we can't complete it? And loads of homework has gone missing from people's bags, it happens all the time, and Pickled Daniels is always there when it does."

"Exactly," shouted Marley excitedly. "See, it makes sense."

"OK, but how come Mrs T has never done anything about it?"

"Yer, don't know. Maybe she doesn't realise. But I think we should do something about it," said Marley.

"Us? What can we do?" replied George frowning.

"Come on, we'd better finish this lap, or Mr Rowlands will go cuckoo crazy." George pulled a silly face.

They started running again and fell silent, both thinking about times in the past when Pickled Daniels could have been the cause of their misery.

"Listen," said George as they neared the group, "don't say anything to anybody about this OK? We don't know what she's up to, and she really scares me. She mustn't know we're on to her. If she hears about it, we're in big trouble."

"Don't worry, she freaks me out. I won't tell a soul. And don't say anything to Phoebe, she'll blab it to the teachers."

"Yer, good point. OK."

They reached the rest of the group, and Mr Rowlands welcomed them back into the team talk. George and Marley stood at the back, they had a lot of thinking to do.

8 WHO WANTS TO SEE ME TOOLS?

Pickled Daniels had risen earlier than usual; the talent show had really thrown her. She wouldn't usually spend her time at home on a Saturday, she preferred to be out in town deliberately tripping up teenagers or coughing on seven-year-olds – an especially favourite pastime.

She had consulted the *Compendium* about the baking club, but now she had the talent show to contend with. She was split on which one was more important to deal with. On the one hand, the talent show was a considerable inconvenience and meant kids running around, screaming and having fun in front of her for hours on end. On the other hand, the baking club was regular, and so she was late every evening it was on. She walked into her living room and took down the *Compendium* from the shelf. Mumbling to herself she flicked through the pages. A small, creased black and white photo flipped out and floated gently to the floor.

"What's that you've given me, something for me to see," she said creaking to pick it up. It was ancient, beaten and crinkled. She gazed at the photo of a young man, her eyes shined brightly as she stared intently at the man staring right back at her. She paused for breath.

"No. No, no, no. Mustn't get distracted by sentimentality, can't think about the past," Pickled Daniels said stuffing the photograph into her pocket. She began to browse through the *Compendium* again, racing through pages.

"Thank you me Darling, you've done stupendous work for Mumsie," she announced to the book. "Pianos, I knew you had it for me treacle, now I may be able to do something about the appalling show. Right, what do I need?" She started scrawling items down on the pad. "Yes me darling, I need a hammer, wire cutters, screwdriver...I think I have all those things, my sweetheart." Pickled Daniels trudged her way into her single connected garage.

Light bounced off the walls illuminating her bright workshop of vile items which she used for tormenting children. On the wall and stored in trunks were a vast array of grizzly tools to help her destroy toys, interrupt games and completely upset science experiments. A whole collection of scissors of different sizes, two large jars of itching powder and sneeze powder, a complete series of drawers containing fake flies, giant spiders, worms and other dreadful insects. Another wall held coiled springs, metal hoops, plastic rings and large hooks just in case she needed to construct some appalling contraption or other.

Pickled Daniels didn't want children to be hurt, she just liked to see them upset and get the awful sprats away from her as quickly as possible, so this was her armoury. Across the other side were pots of goo which could be placed on floors and door handles. Finally, on the far wall, were the stinky cages. A series of immense metal bared cages containing mice, rats, toads, frogs, voles and ferrets. All of them scuttling to and fro in their little dens, the frogs bouncing off the bars in desperation to get out. The mice and rat pens were full to the brim with vermin gnawing at the metal. Pickled Daniels shuffled over to the cages, gently running her hand along the top edge. *The good thing about animals,* thought Pickled Daniels, *is they don't answer back.*

"Quiet me darlings, Mummy's thinking," she murmured. At her workbench, she opened a huge, hefty drawer which was chock full of tools and apparatus. Rummaging through she felt a hammer, she placed it on the work surface then dug deeper into the drawer moving things about and eventually extracting some large wire cutters.

"Here they are," she announced to herself smugly. She raised them up to inspect them closer in the light.

"I think me needs a smaller pair as well," she said addressing the rats in the cage. So again she bent into the enormous trunk and prodded tools scouring for a small pair of wire cutters.

"Must be here somewhere me babies," she said without raising her head. As she poked around in the trunk, she daydreamed about hideous creatures.

Pickled Daniels loved all small animals, from the tiniest ants up to the most enormous rat. She'd found that they were useful on two levels. Either the children hated them, and so they had the desired effect at disrupting whatever was going on, or the teacher had a phobia for something or other and ended up shouting the place down. She remembered fondly the time she'd released two furry ferrets into Mr Savage's classroom only to see him two hours later, on a chair screaming like a little girl while the children shrieked with laughter. This hadn't pleased Pickled Daniels in the slightest, the last thing she needed to hear was thirty children laughing, but overall it had the desired effect. It had taken another hour for Mrs Tinsley to gently talk Mr Savage off the chair assuring him that he wasn't going to be bitten. Half the school had been shut down and it took them two days to find the pests. Eventually, Pickled Daniels had merely collected them in the box as they were hungry (it's hard work for a ferret to scare people for two days). But the children were sent home to allow the council to thoroughly de-fume the school and confirm that no additional vermin could be found. She remembered fondly how she spent a quiet afternoon reading in the school hall without so much as the murmur of tiny voices to disturb her, *pure bliss*.

Finally, she located the wire cutters at the bottom corner of the trunk, her back gave a loud crack as she straightened up. Pickled Daniels was getting old, and all this business of terrifying children was hard on the body, especially on a Saturday. *She was ready for action.*

Pickled Daniels took a small swig of dark rum while searching for the school keys, her eyes glazing over. The building had over fifty doors, the key set was enormous. Pickled Daniels wobbled lazily across the playground towards the school, wheezing as she went, half dragging the bag of tools. With the keys gentling jangling against her side Pickled Daniels looked like a decrepit jailer. She hunted for the correct key then let herself in. Nothing beat going to the school on a Saturday or Sunday: no children! She carefully locked the door behind her.

Discreetly peering around, she double-checked that no one was there, lumbering into the school hall. She couldn't help think about what Mrs Tinsley had said about retiring. Perhaps it would be better to not have to spend the weekend thinking about disgusting, cheerful children. But it was her job, and deep down she loved to think about ingenious and yet subtle ways of upsetting them; how could she do that if she retired! She'd have to spend all her time at supermarkets and shopping centres wiping her bogeys on children's toys like she had to some Saturdays when there was nothing else to do. And that's not a life thought Pickled Daniels.

Pickled Daniels spotted the upright piano.

"There you are my beauty," she muttered to herself now feeling the effects of her rum, tripping slightly on the flat floor. Reaching the piano, she dropped the tool bag and leaned against it, catching her breath. She bent down to see how she should proceed, the world spinning a little around her. Over the years Pickled Daniels had learnt so much about taking musical instruments to pieces she could have made a career out of instrument repairs. Instead, she'd become adept at removing parts to make 'adjustments' then refitting as if nothing had happened, rendering the instrument wholly inoperable and almost un-repairable in most cases. It was far more satisfying.

She laid out her gruesome array of tools like a doctor about to perform a complicated surgical procedure. Gulping her rum she lifted the top of the piano and peered in, she could see the complex arrangement of strings, nuts and the massive striking mechanism. She crouched under the keyboard, lifted a screwdriver and began to gently tease off the front of the piano. Eventually, she removed the panel, revealing the very heart of the instrument. Pickled Daniels whistled happily.

Was that noise? She stopped and lay entirely still like she was taking part in a game of musical statues. Was that the jangle of keys in a door lock? She inched around the piano then paused, straining to listen for the sound. Then she heard it, the unmistakable echo of Mrs Tinsley's footsteps in the dim distance. Click, clack, click, clack, click, clack... as her high heels struck the glistening surfaces of the hallway, accompanied by the padding of four tiny feet. *What shall I do?* The colour drained from her cheeks. She glanced around the room trying to conjure up an escape plan.

Desperately she pulled herself up, gathering her tools, wincing each time they struck each other, making a terrible noise. "Shhh, shhh," she whispered.

The sound of footsteps was getting louder and louder as they approached.

"Breath deeply me sweetheart. Nothing to worry about, nothing to worry about".

She was shaking now as she pulled at her tools and feeling a little drunk. Sweat dripped off her brow.

Then it happened. Turning, one of her feet caught the edge of the bottle, with a crash it fell sending brown liquid snaking across the floor.

"Arrrggghhhhhhhh..........".

She silently screamed, her face screwed up in anguish. She slumped to the floor, not sure what to do next.

9 CLIVE'S FEELING A LITTLE SICK

Mrs Tinsley wasn't having a good morning. Her dearly beloved pet Chihuahua, Clive, had been sick all over the kitchen. Mrs T had a strict Saturday morning routine which she didn't like to have disturbed - it went something like this.

6.30AM Alarm goes off, allowing her to wake gradually to the sound of Radio 4.

6.45AM Nudge Gerald (Mrs Tinsley's husband) to get him out of bed.

7.04AM Gerald arrives with a beautiful, fresh cup of coffee.

7.06AM Turn over and go back to sleep.

8.10AM Wake up to find a cold cup of coffee on the bedside table.

8.12AM Nudge Gerald again. Check Gerald has taken Clive for a walk.

8.20AM Shout at Gerald (could be for various reasons).

8.25AM Gerald brings breakfast in bed.

8.30AM Gerald runs a bath.

8.33AM Shout at Gerald (could be for various

reasons).

8.35AM Get in bath and demand Gerald bring morning paper.

8.40AM Start reading paper in bath.

8.50AM Shout at Gerald (could be for various reasons)

9.30AM Get out of bath and dry. Blow dry hair and apply make-up.

10.30AM Cuddle Clive and shout at Gerald (could be for various reasons).

On this particular Saturday, the plan didn't really go as forecast. At 8.43 between getting in the bath and reading the paper - and before she had had a chance to shout at Gerald for the fourth time - she'd heard him screaming downstairs. In a panic, Mrs T resorted to getting out of the bath herself (without Gerald standing and holding her towel as he usually would) and rushed downstairs dripping water everywhere.

She'd found Gerald in the kitchen, Clive standing next to him, with sick all over the kitchen floor.

"What's wrong with him, Gerald?" demanded Mrs Tinsley, scooping Clive up. "What's wrong with little Clivy Wivy," she said giving him a little stroke.

"It might have been the cold chicken I gave

him earlier from the fridge," said Gerald.

Mrs Tinsley exploded. "That chicken's been in there two weeks, I told you to get rid of it."

Mrs Tinsley had switched into head teacher mode while scolding him.

She returned her attention to stroking Clive.

"Daddy's been very naughty and will clear it up for you," she said and marched out to the kitchen clinging onto a bewildered Clive.

It wasn't the start to the day she'd wanted. She had to go the school to start the preparations for the talent show. But climbing the stairs with a sick dog didn't put her in a jovial mood for it. And so it was that when Mrs Tinsley entered the school that morning, she was feeling decidedly grumpy.

Pickled Daniels was in a dire panic, it was definitely the unmistakable sound of Mrs Tinsley walking through the school with her mutt Clive. She had to act. Quick. She must have given the game away now she thought to herself, the clanking of the tools were just too loud to conceal. *But what about the drink on the floor?*

This was the school hall, one of the primary school rules was "**No fizzy drinks in the hall**." She spent many an afternoon cleaning the floor after she had deliberately spilt water and blamed it on a child wetting themselves, but now here was evidence that she was the culprit for once. And what was worse it smelt so strong!

The footsteps stopped. Was that Mrs T going into her office or was she about to enter the hall? Pickled Daniels froze, scared to even breath. She had an awful, prickly feeling in her stomach. The room was silent. She waited, stuck to the floor like a fly in a glue factory. She'd been still so long she thought perhaps she'd imagined the footsteps.

Clive is definitely not well, thought Mrs Tinsley as she sat behind her desk. She put him on her lap while she reviewed the talent show paperwork, poking him every now and then like a knowledgeable vet. She had various council forms to fill in and needed to plan the evening thoroughly as the date was fast approaching. She fired up the computer and leaned back in her chair while it slowly got going. She listened to the faint sound of birds in the trees as she looked out across the school field, enjoying the quiet.

There were some advantages to coming to school on a Saturday; she could get on with her work in peace without being disturbed by all the other teachers. Mrs Tinsley's large desk had portraits of her husband, Clive and the Queen on it. Around the walls hung several certificates between bookshelves and in one corner near the window, two sets of filing cabinets. On top of the cabinets were her prized collection of royal wedding mugs, cups and saucers from every royal wedding since Queen Victoria. Mrs T surveyed the room with pride.

"Do you like being with Mummy at her work?" she said to Clive while rubbing his belly. Clive seemed fairly nonchalant on the subject.

"Did Daddy make you sick?"

Pickled Daniels unfroze and decided she had to do something about the liquid on the hall floor. Slowly removing her shawl, the most ghastly whiff of body odour escaped around the hall. She heard Clive yapping from the head's office and relaxed a little. Mrs T wasn't about to walk in. She covered the wet patch with the clothing, then mopped it up with her hands, moving the shawl in a circle. Her head span. The liquid stunk, but Pickled Daniels didn't notice. Moving backwards she collided with her bag of tools, sending the giant wire cutters tumbling onto the hammer with an almighty *clunk*.

In Mrs T's office Clive pricked up his ears, and even Mrs T couldn't miss the noise.

"What was that Clive?"

They both sat still, listening. Mrs T rose, and Clive dropped to the floor. Clive didn't feel so sick now, he liked a bit of excitement every now and then. Mrs T exited with Clive in tow – searching for the source of the noise.

Pickled Daniels was blindly gathering tools, stuffing them into her bag. The click-clack of Mrs T's shoes echoed. They were getting louder. Thankfully the shawl had done the job and soaked most of the liquid up. She shook it out from the wet ball it had become and put it back on. It dripped a little. She pulled the tools to one side and was bending down to put the cover on the piano when the hall door swung open, revealing Mrs T and Clive standing in the entrance like a couple of mismatched gladiators, the lighting shining behind them.

"What on earth is going on Mrs Daniels?" demanded Mrs T, striding across the hall. Pickled Daniels spluttered. Mrs T got the unmistakable smell of alcohol up her nose. Clive got a whiff of it too, whimpering.

"Well?" Mrs T had to stop breathing through

her nose, the smell invading her nostrils.

"Mrs Tinsley, I...I...I can explain," Pickled Daniels stammered.

"I hope you can Mrs Daniels," barked Mrs T. "As you know we have strict rules on hours of working and who is allowed in the school during the weekend, I gave no sanction of additional paid overtime this weekend. You should have finished cleaning hours ago."

Pickled Daniels thought quickly. She knew how to manipulate Mrs T when she wanted to.

"You sees Mrs Tinsley," Pickled Daniels had an idea forming in her mind. "You sees Mrs Tinsley I've been worried about this old piano for a long time." Mrs T's face softened. Pickled Daniel's knew she was getting somewhere now, she carried on with her passionate speech. "And when you mentioned about that lovely talent show you wanted to put on I was worried see that maybe the day you came to the show, it wouldn't work, can you imagine the disappointment for the dear children if that happened? I didn't want to disturb you, you see. So I thought to meself, I must check the piano and perhaps give it a little oil and maintenance. It's used every day, and so I thought Saturday would be the best day. I don't want money, Mrs Tinsley, I'm just happy to work for nothing if it makes the children happy. That's why I'm here today you see, to make sure everything is just right for you. The children mean so much to me."

Pickled Daniels finished her speech, her bottom lip wobbling. She knew she'd done it. During her appeal, Mrs T had wilted.

"Well...well....erm… yes... that's excellent thinking Mrs Daniels." Mrs T was clearly impressed. "All I would suggest is that you ask for my permission before doing anything like this in the future."

"Yes Mrs Tinsley, of course." Pickled Daniels bent down to give Clive a little stroke as if the gesture would clear the air. Clive was having none of it and nipped at her fingers.

"We're very lucky to have such a warm-hearted person around the school. Have you finished with the piano?"

Clearly, Pickled Daniels would have to come up with a new plan, she couldn't sabotage the piano now.

"Yes, just got to replace the front and we is all done."

"Good, then you can go. Come on Clive, time to get back." Clive turned and took a growl at Pickled Daniels.

"Oh, and Mrs Daniels. I did notice that maybe your shawl needs a little clean. I think you've spilt something down it," called Mrs T from the door.

"Thank you Mrs Tinsley," replied Pickled Daniels waving, a massive drop plopping from her shawl.

Pickled Daniels slumped to the floor. Beaten. She sat thinking for a few minutes before slowly gathering her tools, she had to ready another plan. And quickly......

10 MEET THE BOFFIN

George's cousin was called Sam. She was fifteen and lived with George's auntie Nicola. Sam attended the local college and had one ambition in life - to become a computer programmer, or "boffin" as George's dad called her. She told George she wanted to work for one of the large computer games companies, writing reams of computer code and bringing her own fantasy worlds alive.

George didn't see Sam that often, fifteen-year-old girls don't always like hanging around with eleven-year-old boys. But they did have one thing in common, some weekends George could be found around Sam's house playing computer games. Sam had one of the best bedrooms George had ever seen. Actually, **it was** the best bedroom he'd ever seen. She was always working, always learning, which George loved. The major problem was communicating with Sam, she spoke so fast that George had trouble keeping up.

As they approached Sam's road, George tried

to explain this to Marley.

"What do you mean fast?" said Marley.

"I mean like this really fast." George spat out the sentence.

"What, like this?" said Marley at break-neck speed.

"Yes, like that," said George equally quickly. They laughed.

"So why are we coming again?" said Marley, returning to average speed.

"'Cause Sam will know what to do. My Dad says she's the brainiest one in the family and that she knows a lot of stuff," said George. "And who else can we tell about Pickled Daniels? Can't say anything to my mum and dad, or your mum and dad, or Phoebe. And Uncle Ernie's deaf, but Sam will know what to do. I hope." George gulped.

"I hope so too." Marley sighed.

George pressed the doorbell. There was no movement inside.

"Must be out," said Marley turning to go.

"Wait a minute." George pulled Marley's jumper. "Sam can never hear the door as she's normally programming or something. She has the doorbell connected to the Internet which sends her a message, and it pops up on her screen. She'll be down soon."

They waited for another minute before they heard a door slam upstairs and then spied a whirlwind rushing down the stairs. The front door snapped open. Sam began speaking very fast.

"Hello, George. How are you? You all right? What's going on? Who's this?" She eventually took a breath.

"Hi Sam, this is Marley, my friend."

"Cool, come in then." She sprinted back up the stairs leaving the door wide open.

"That's normal," explained George smiling. "We'd better go in."

"Come on then," shouted Sam from upstairs.

As they reached the top of the stairs, Marley saw Sam's room. He couldn't miss it, the door was bright green and sprayed on in bold, gold letters were SAM. Marley could hear muffled sounds from inside, as though a whole army were in battle.

"Ready?" said George before they walked in.

"Ready for what?" asked Marley.

Instead of answering George pushed the door open. To Marley, it was like falling into a different dimension. The volume was overwhelming. Marley stood in the middle of the room with his mouth open, spellbound.

It was dark except for the light from the three large flat screens on the gargantuan desk. On it were two keyboards, a pink mouse, two joysticks, two steering wheels, a pair of 3D glasses, a games pad and controllers. Nearby there was a towering bookshelf with hundreds of computer magazines, neatly filed in chronological order, plus all the latest computer programming books.

Sam focused on the three screens which showed a bright desert scene in chaos, animated soldiers ran in and out of burnt out jeeps and buildings and others jumped from trees. All around gunfire blasted. Screaming came from one side of the room as the speakers beat out a real-time battle scene. Above the noise of commanders shouting orders was a pulsating music track. On the centre screen was Sam's character, she was controlling it with joysticks in each hand plus she had an earpiece and microphone neatly around her head.

"OK, Ellie, cover me while I move to the palm tree. On the count of three...one, two, three." Sam spoke into her microphone, ignoring them both.

Marley studied the room. He'd never seen anything like it in his life. There were so many electronics, drawings, papers and doodles strewn over the place. Each wall had a large speaker, throwing sound out, so the noise came from everywhere.

George stood patiently next to Sam, watching the action on the screen. Marley sat on the bed all the while admiring the fantastic room around him. Finally, Sam's character came to rest behind a wall.

"Hey Ellie, my cousin has turned up. Got to go." She blurted into the microphone. She pressed P on the keyboard, and the room fell silent.

Marley started fidgeting with his fingers, the silence seemed to surround him.

"This room is soooo good," said Marley in awe.

"Yer, it's great isn't it," replied George.

Sam spun round on her chair, picked her legs up and sat cross-legged putting her face in her hands. Staring directly at Marley.

"So you two, what's going on? Assume you both want to play some games?" Marley looked at George for support, he was slightly flustered. Thankfully George took control of the situation.

"No," said George. "We actually came for some advice. We didn't know who else to talk to."

"Advice, from me? Really?" Sam smiled a little.

"Yes, if that's all right?"

"Go on, shoot then," said Sam readjusting her position. She picked up a pencil and paper with her hand poised above the page like a seasoned newspaper reporter ready to take some notes.

"OK." George took a deep breath and looked at Marley for support. "This is going to sound a little weird, right. We have a cleaner at school. She's called Pickled Daniels. She's really, really old and doesn't smell that nice at all. She's also incredibly horrible and nasty, and we think she's been messing up some of our work."

"Messing it up? What do you mean?" Sam scribbled feverishly.

"For instance. We do science experiments one day and then come in the next day, and something has gone wrong with them. Or we find our coats have somehow fallen into a cleaning bucket. Or that some of the good gym equipment has broken. We don't know, but we think she's been doing stuff to it, she's always nearby when something happens. And we think she bullies the year ones. She's making everyone's life a misery in the school, but the teachers don't see it.". George took a breath, happy to have finally told someone.

"Mmmm..." Sam began pacing, tapping her nose with the pencil.

Marley chimed in, "Yer, and she's always there at baking club when the ovens stop working or in the canteen when the salt has been replaced by sugar."

Sam spun around. "So what can I do about it?" she said at normal speed for once.

"Erm, I don't know. Just thought you might have some ideas for us?" George replied, his shoulders slumping.

"Let me think." Sam sat back down and span in her chair, gazing at the ceiling. Marley stared at Sam, his heart racing.

George glanced at Marley, smiling to himself.

Sam kept spinning round and round going faster and faster. It seemed to go on for an eternity before Sam stopped and closed her eyes tapping the pencil on the side of the chair. Another few minutes passed in silence.

Suddenly she opened her eyes and spun round to face her desk. She pulled her chair right up to the keyboard, back straight like a brigadier general poised for battle plans.

"OK. Got it." She tapped on the keyboard at

a rate of knots. Marley had never seen someone type so fast in his life. The three monitors burst into life, and each of them began to churn computer code. "So, you really think she's doing stuff, and you want to prove what she's doing, right?"

"Well...I suppose so...we hadn't really thought about it like that. But yes, I suppose if we can prove something..." George looked at Marley. Marley nodded his head.

"Yer, if we had proof or something we could show Mrs T or Mr Savage," added Marley.

"Right. So how can we prove it? We need to set something up and see what this Pickled Daniels does. Is there anything special coming up at school in the next few weeks? You said she enjoyed breaking things or messing things up, so she's bound to get annoyed if anything special is happening."

Before they could say a word, Sam had frantically worked on her keyboard and the school website popped up on the central monitor. Two words sprang from the screen: TALENT SHOW.

"That's it," exclaimed Sam. "If she's as vile as you said she won't like that. Not at all. She'll want to mess it up."

Sam moved to different websites, typing furiously as she worked. Her head darted between the three monitors while she searched for something. George and Marley sat quietly reviewing the screens.

"Won't be long," she said over her shoulder, still tapping away.

Marley looked at the wall over Sam's bed, it was covered in photos of her and her friends from school and holidays; it looked like she had a lot of fun. In one snap Sam was smiling directly at the camera with three of her friends piled in behind her, squeezing each other out of the photograph. Marley smiled, he hoped he had friends like that when he was fifteen.

"Right, this is it." Sam's screen was full of code. It looked like a load of random numbers and letters to George and Marley.

"What's that?" George asked.

"CCTV for the school," stated Sam, proudly.

"CCTV - what's that?". Marley frowned.

"It stands for Closed Circuit Television. Have you ever noticed that some areas of the school have cameras in the corner of the rooms or outside? It's for the security system, but it's never really used. Look it says here where they are." She poked at the screen. "I've just hacked into the internal website for the local council so we can see it. But I can't get any further without getting into loads of trouble."

"We don't want to get in trouble," said Marley. "We don't even know if Pickled Daniels is really up to anything. This is silly."

"No, look, it lists the camera positions in the school, and if we can somehow get into the website, we could look at the cameras and then somehow record them if Pickled Daniels was doing anything out of hours. They put these camera systems into schools to detract burglars, but no one ever looks at what's recorded."

"I don't understand," said Marley. His head buzzing.

"Doesn't matter," said Sam. "All you need to know is that there are cameras in the school and somewhere they are keeping a record of the footage."

"That's great," said George. "If we could place something in front of the cameras and then see if Pickled Daniels does something to it we could prove she was messing things up for us."

"Exactly." Sam lounged back in the chair with her legs on the desk, like a contented lizard.

"OK, but you can't get into the website," said Marley. "So that doesn't help us."

"All I need is the code," said Sam casually.

"What's that?" asked Marley.

"It says here," Sam prodded a finger at the screen, "Headteacher log in details. Please sign in using your school password provided by the council. But I think I can get round this. I just need a few days, and I should have direct access. Oh, and we need something to keep copies of the videos on for easy display. You two got smartphones?"

George looked at Marley, both shook their heads.

"OK, get your Dad's then George, and we'll put it on that. I can hack into the phone and create an app where we can record all the evidence. Easy. You can then watch what Pickled Daniels is up to on his phone."

"I'm not sure if I can borrow my dad's phone, I don't think he'd agree. But if we can get it that's a great plan. We can show Mrs Tinsley what we've found from his phone." George said.

"Yer, your basically ask us to steal his phone," Marley said.

"Not steal Marley, borrow for a while. It will be fine. You guys will figure it out. OK, I've got to get on with my game. But we have a plan. So let's say you come back here next weekend with your dad's phone and we'll get it set up. We don't want to lose any time, you must get it to me as soon as you can. Oh. And try to think of setting something up which is so tempting for Pickled Daniels to mess with, she won't be able to resist."

Marley gawped at George for support, but George had a big grin on his face.

"I suppose it could work, we've just got to make sure we get my dad's phone," George said rising to leave.

"Exactly. And make sure you can set up whatever you think of in front of one of the cameras, or it's a waste of time."

Sam put on her wireless headset. "All set Ellie." With a quick press on the keyboard, the three screens flicked onto the desert scene, and the room was a war zone again.

George and Marley crept out the room leaving the sound of gunfire behind.

11 WATCH MY SISTER DISAPPEAR

It was Sunday, and George wanted to spend the day working on his baking magic trick. He decided to try a find out precisely what had been done in the past and everything to do with magic. He had a lot on his mind, he had to get his dad's phone for Sam, but he was going to put it off as long as possible like he frequently did with homework.

It was only seven in the morning, and it was Dad's lie-in day so he knew that he wouldn't surface till after ten, even mum stayed in bed until eight. Phoebe was already up, standing in the centre of the living room dressed in a bright green Tutu, complimented with an orange top – like a dancing carrot.

"What are you doing?" George demanded. The TV was on silently in the corner. Phoebe didn't take her eyes off it; she was mimicking some dance moves.

"I'm practising my ballet," replied Phoebe. Phoebe desperately wanted to win the talent show so had been rehearsing every day for the last week. It's not every day you get the opportunity to win a years supply of sweets. She had decided to complete an elaborate dance sequence from her mum's DVD copy of a Russian theatre company's *Swan Lake*. It was one of the most famous ballet productions, and Phoebe thought that this would impress the judges (and her mum). Though she was finding it somewhat challenging to imitate a professional dancer with years of experience.

George was secretly cross, he didn't want his sister to be this enthusiastic about the talent show. It was his chance to shine, and she was stealing the limelight from him. Not only that - he desperately wanted to win the sweets all for himself.

"I wanted to watch the TV, you'll have to stop," said George lunging for the remote control.

"Hey, that's not fair," said Phoebe spinning round and jumping towards the remote too. They scrabbled around the floor wrestling like two squirrels at a nut market.

"I'll call Dad," said Phoebe calmly.

They stopped in a tangle of limbs. "Don't," said George. Calling Dad on a Sunday morning was a complete no, no.

"Stop it then, let me have the remote," said Phoebe calmly.

George didn't let go.

"**Dadddddddddddddddddddddddd ddd**," said Phoebe in a whisper.

"All right, have it," said George flinging the remote onto the sofa as he stormed out of the room. Phoebe started the DVD again, smirking to herself.

George wandered into the kitchen, opening the family laptop. Waiting for it to start he helped himself to some cereal. Slowly munching he did a search on YouTube for magic tricks, he was bombarded with thousands of options, most of them card tricks. *That's just dull* thought George, I need something more exciting, something to really thrill the crowd. He carried on searching and then typed in 'learning magic'. Again the list was endless, but something caught his eye. A video titled 'Watch my sister disappear'. George laughed *if only he could*! He clicked on it and a boy about his age dressed in a bright green shirt and red waistcoat holding a large sheet appeared. George guessed it was from America as the boy was stood in front of a gigantic fridge. The boy began talking in a thick American accent, so he knew he was right.

"Hi, welcome to my magic channel, on today's show I'm going to make my little sister disappear." From one side of the screen stepped a girl holding a giant pink lollipop. For a little sister, she was quite big!

"Hi," she said waving to the camera.

"Right, stand over there," whispered the magician to his sister, pushing her to one side of the kitchen. He fumbled about with a large yellow sheet which had an American football team emblem blazoned across it. Eventually, he picked it up for the camera and came round in front of his sister.

"Step back," he prodded his sister again forcing her to move backwards, obviously getting annoyed. George was enjoying this, he scooped up another spoonful of cereal to crunch on while watching.

"My assistant will simply disappear before your eyes, including her magic lollipop." George thought that the lollipop was probably not magic, so this didn't really make any sense, but he went along with it anyway.

The magician stepped in front of the camera. Pulling the sheet up - his sister was slowly covered. Finally, all that was left was her pink tubby face and the very tip of the lollipop above the cloth. The magician pulled the sheet up and down a couple of times, demonstrating they were still there, and then covered them completely.

He counted down and then threw the sheet into the air, it flopped to the floor in a heap. He placed his hands in the air as if to say 'look at this.' His sister had disappeared. George stopped munching and stared at the screen. *How did they do that?* He was impressed. The boy stood for a few seconds, bowing to the camera. From the side of the kitchen, his sister leaned into the frame again, killing the illusion. The magician went mad, pushing her out, screaming at the top of his voice. George nearly choked on his cereal, this was one of the funniest magic shows he'd ever seen.

Making things disappear and reappear appealed to George. If he could build on that and perhaps introduce some baking, he might just win the talent show. George finished his cereal and then sat thinking through his options. It would be difficult to get an oven onto the stage so what about making raw cakes into cooked ones in an instant, through magic. That's it! All I need to do is bake some cakes the day before then use these as the final 'cooked' ones. The whole idea was taking shape, he imagined the school crowd rising to their feet and clapping wildly as he magically baked his cakes in an instant. This is going to be great thought George! I will be crowned talent show winner and master baker magician all on one night, not to mention the year's supply of sweets he would win! He couldn't wait, all he had to do now was practice.

12 THE MAGIC BOX

George was pulled from his daydream when Uncle Ernie wandered into the kitchen.

"Morning lad," said Ernie carrying the Sunday paper under his arms. He sat down at the kitchen table and spread out the newspaper, coughing as he did so.

"Erm, Uncle Ernie?" said George nervously fiddling with thin air.

"Yes lad," replied Ernie, he continued to delve through the various sections, not bothering to look up.

"I was just about to cook, I needed the table for my ingredients," said George.

"Book," said Ernie. "You're reading a book you say? Good lad. When I was your age, I'd already read the complete works of Shakespeare and was well on the way to completing War and Peace."

George didn't really know what Ernie was going on about so just nodded intelligently at him. Ernie carried on blindly searching through the newspaper sending large sections of it floating through the air.

George sighed. I'll have to work around him he thought. Removing a cookbook from the shelf, he selected a cake recipe. Parading around the kitchen, he picked up bowls, scales, a spoon and jugs ready for use. George wanted to practice as if he was on stage at the show so it was essential to have everything lined up ready to go as it would be on the day.

Perhaps Ernie is useful for something thought George, I'll pretend he's the audience. Squeezing everything up to the other side of the table, he was now facing Ernie. Ernie was oblivious to him and even let out a small fart, George grimaced and tried not to breathe in for a while.

When he was ready, George stood at the table as if facing the audience and began to rehearse his act.

"Ladies and Gentlemen, I am George, the world's first baking magician." He stopped, he didn't think the announcement had enough gravity. Perhaps my voice is too high thought George. He cleared his throat and began again, putting on a deeper voice. **"Ladies and Gentlemen, it gives me pleasure to present the world's first baking magic trick**." Ernie looked up now.

"What's this?"

"It's my talent show act, Ernie," said George, frustrated by the distraction.

"Oh. Very good, carry on then." Ernie leaned back and folded his arms ready for the impromptu show.

George hadn't anticipated Ernie being interested in watching him so this was slightly unnerving. Carrying on regardless, he worked through the show starting with mixing the ingredients in an exaggerated way as George thought a magician would. Ernie sat silently through the whole thing, he even nodded and smiled at the appropriate times. Finally, George got to the point in the show where he was meant to magically make the cooked ones appear in an instant.

"This is where I make them instantly baked," said George explaining the process to Ernie, "so I'll have some already cooked and I'll make them appear in place of these ones." George pointed to the uncooked lumps of cake in their holders.

"What!" shouted Ernie, cupping his ear. "Didn't hear you lad."

"I said, this is where I have some already prepared cooked ones and then they will magically appear here," repeated George, waving his hand above the cakes to show where he meant.

"What do you mean booked?"

"No Ernie, cooked," said George louder.

"Oh, cooked, that makes sense," said Ernie now grasping the situation. "How do you do that then?"

George deflated. "I'm not sure, I hadn't thought of that," he said. They both looked at the raw cake mixture in silence. George scratching his head. Then Ernie piped up.

"What about I make you a magic box?" said Ernie grinning. "That would make it easy."

"What...what's that?" replied George, confused.

"Well," Ernie said. "In my youth, I used to help out a magician on the weekend. He did kid's parties. Good money that was, I can tell you. The magic is all done by mirrors you see. He used to have a table with a secret surface under one side where he could store bits and bobs. If he wanted them to appear, he used a little handle on the inside and pull it. Then the mirrors would move, the audience sees the items on the top from a different angle so it would look like they had suddenly…...well magically I suppose....appeared in place of the other thing. Easy that is. So I could make you a box with that in it. You could use it for your show. Then you put your cooked cakes inside and then at the right moment pull the handle, and you'd be magic." Ernie sat back on his chair folding his arms, looking satisfied with himself.

George just looked at him. Usually, Ernie just kept himself to himself and George had nothing to do with him. This was the first time he'd realised they might have something in common.

"That sounds great Ernie." George smiled. "That would really help me. I could put your box straight on the table with the cooked ones in it, distract the audience with a wave of my stick…" he mimed moving a magic wand above an imaginary box, "…then that would be it, they just materialise."

Dad arrived at the kitchen door rubbing his hair like an itchy ferret and surveyed the carnage in front of him.

"Morning George, morning Ernie." He moved to fill up the kettle, yawning in the process. "What you doing? This is a right mess." It was a valid question given the ingredients covering the table and newspapers strewn all over the floor.

"The lad was showing me his magic," said

Ernie.

"Yer Dad, Ernie said he could build a magic box to help with the show," said George proudly.

Phoebe pranced into the kitchen in her sickening, green Tutu singing to herself - spinning gently.

"Phoebe I'm talking to Dad and Ernie, you'll have to go into the living room," said George curtly.

Phoebe ignored him and continued strutting around the kitchen.

"Ernie is going to help George with his talent show," Dad said to Phoebe as he made a cup of tea.

"That's not fair," Phoebe whined. "Can't someone help me as well?"

"Well," said Dad thinking about it, his brow furrowed in concentration. "Perhaps Ernie could make you a new tutu with a colour which won't make the audience sick?." Dad guffawed. "Or what about I sing with you?". He stood, feet apart like an experienced opera singer. A deep-throated bellow of Nessun Dorma came out. It wasn't really singing, it sounded more like an elderly hippo crying.

"You are not singing with me," said Phoebe, mortified at the prospect of her Dad singing like that in front of anyone! Her face screwed up into a quiver. "I don't need any help." She stormed out of the kitchen, stamping her feet extra loud.

"Well you can't please everyone," Dad said grinning, sitting down at the table with his tea.

13 THE OLD APRON

It was Monday (the most horrible day!) morning again. The days till the appalling talent show were ticking down. They were planning to have a discussion about the decoration and general arrangements for the show. Pickled Daniels was dreading it.

"Ah, there you are Mrs Daniels," Mrs T gushed. "I'm just looking at what colour we should use for the stage backdrop. What do you think?" She held a range of coloured material samples, moving them up to the light in front of the stage. Pickled Daniels had no idea at all. She liked black, but Mrs T didn't have a black sample.

"What do you think the youngest children would like," Pickled Daniels said, trying to sound sincere, buttering up Mrs T.

"Yes, that's very thoughtful Mrs Daniels, we should make it bright for the youngest ones. Let's go with yellow then." She held up the yellow sample proudly, admiring it at arm's length.

"Good, that's settled. Now front curtains. Are they still operating correctly?"

"I needs to give him a little grease, that's all. They should be working." Pickled Daniels murmured picking at an invisible thread on her clothes.

"Good, very good." Mrs T wasn't even listening, she was on to the next thing. "And chairs Mrs Daniels, do we have enough chairs? I'm expecting a lot of parents for this show. It'll be one of the major school fundraisers for the year. The children find it very inspirational. They seem to be at their happiest at these sort of events."

Pickled Daniels gulped back a wave of nausea, her face turned grey.

"There's enough good chairs. Mrs Tinsley…I was thinking…sometimes I gets one of me headaches in the evening, especially if I've had a long day. And this show will be a lot of work. Perhaps after I've helped set-up, I don't need to be here on the actual evening of the show…"

There was a pause, she thought that Mrs T might be about to agree. He eyes drilled into her.

"Nonsense," said Mrs T sternly. "I'll need you here. There's too much to do, and anyway, the children love seeing you around the school. They know they can rely on you to help out." Mrs T changed tack slightly. "Well, that brings me onto the subject again Mrs Daniels. I wanted to talk to you again about the dreaded *retirement* word. Are you finding the job difficult, neither of us are getting any younger, and you are past the age of official retirement? If you're getting more of these headaches, perhaps it's time to hang up the old apron. I certainly will be in a couple of years."

"No...no," replied Pickled Daniels, weakly.

"Well, let's hear no more talk about not attending then Mrs Daniels. With so many children and parents in the school at the same time, I'll need you here from early morning until last thing at night. You might even have to help out looking after the reception class. I suggest you take a long break at lunchtime, so you are fully refreshed for the afternoon and evening."

Pickled Daniels paled. A full school of children backstage at a show. It didn't bear thinking about. They would all be so joyful and there'd be laughing, shouting and screaming with pleasure. She could picture it now. I can't let it happen she thought, staring into middle distance.

"Are you OK, Mrs Daniels?"

Pickled Daniels snapped out of her daydream. "Sorry, yes. I...I just imagined how lovely the show will be for the children. They'll be overjoyed." Pickled Daniels faked a big smile. It actually hurt her to hold it.

"You are so right Mrs Daniels. What a lovely thought. You really are so thoughtful sometimes. It will be both enjoyable and thought-provoking for the children. It's useful in giving them confidence and structure to perform and practice for this sort of show." She paused, nodding earnestly. "Very good, you seem to have everything under control Mrs Daniels. I'll write a list to confirm everything which needs doing the week before and on the day in the hall. I'll let you review that and then you can work through it during the week of the show. Is that OK?"

Pickled Daniels nodded weakly, her head a little woozy.

"Good." Mrs T left Pickled Daniels standing alone in front of the stage.

Pickled Daniels laid her hands on the stage, her face in a scowl. How did she get into this position? Her mind was searching desperately for ways to stop the show before it had even begun. *What if some of the grease from the curtain rails happened to get onto the stage* she thought running her hand over it, it would be too slippery to perform on. No, too obvious. She looked around the room at the walls, ceiling and lights. Electrics. *What if the electrics failed*? Perhaps in the middle of the afternoon before the show. What could Mrs T do about that? Nothing. Definitely an option she thought. *Or what about a toad infestation under the stage*? Pickled Daniels thought about how many toads she had in her cages, it just might work. She'd come up with something, the show simply had to be stopped – by whatever means possible.

14 WHO CAN DEMONSTRATE REAL TALENT?

On Wednesday evening, Marley bounced up to George's front door and rang the bell. George's mum answered.

"Hello Marley, how are you?" She smiled. She was always pleased to see Marley.

"Fine thanks," Marley replied, a look of complete blankness on his face. "Is George in?"

"Yes, he's in his room, you can go up."

Marley took off his shoes and made for the stairs.

"What's your act for the show?" George's mum asked before he could get up the stairs.

Marley turned, his cheeks reddened. "Well, my mum said that I should demonstrate all the knots that I've learnt to tie in cubs but my dad said that might be boring for an audience to watch. Then my mum said what about answering some maths questions on stage, cause I'm quite good at maths. But my dad started shouting and said when have you ever seen someone answering maths questions in a talent show on TV, he said my mum was silly, and I couldn't do that. Then my mum said that my Dad was silly as he had left school at sixteen, and she didn't know why she had married someone who couldn't add up. Then my Dad started talking about what his friends down the pub had called my mum, and they had a big argument about it." George's mum nodded and gave Marley a sympathetic smile.

"In the end, my dad said I had to do something which demonstrated real talent," Marley continued. "He said I should do some jokes or something, but I don't know many jokes. So I'm going to juggle with five balls instead."

"Well, that will show real talent," George's mum said. "I'm impressed. How long have you been juggling?"

"I don't know how to juggle." Marley's shoulders slumped, and he headed up the stairs to find George.

"Well...good luck anyway," George's mum shouted at his departing feet.

George was already in front of the computer, rearranging the speakers and microphone.

"Is it working?" Marley sat on the edge of the bed.

"Yes, I just did a test call, and that was all right." George fiddled with the computer. "How's the juggling practice?" George asked, not taking his eyes off the screen.

"It's OK. I can pass one ball from the left hand to my right hand now."

"That's great." George smiled to himself. "You've only got to get the other four balls in the air at the same time then."

"Exactly what my dad said," Marley said, oblivious to the sarcasm.

"I think we have some action," George said sitting back, clicking on some icons. The screen flashed green for a second, the camera sparked into life showing their faces. To make sure Marley raised his hand in the air behind George and it was duplicated on the screen.

"Right, I'll click on Sam now," George said.

The speakers buzzed as the two computers linked. Finally, the ring was interrupted, Sam's grinning face filled the monitor.

"Hey, George. How's it going?" Sam munched on a chocolate bar.

"We're fine thanks. Marley's here too." Marley stuck his hand in the air and waved in the background. Marley's heart beat a little faster.

"Cool. Hi Marley. So, how did you get on in Baking Club last night? Any action from the dreaded Pickled Daniels?"

"We didn't have it. Club was called off as the ovens had stopped working due to a birds nest or something in the chimney. Mrs Walker said that Pickled Daniels was meant to be getting someone to clear it."

"We're sure she made it up. Mrs Walker didn't even check, and Pickled Daniels was grinning when Mrs Walker told us all." Marley piped up.

"Oh…OK. An update from me," said Sam at speed. " I've done some more digging, and there is no way I can hack into those camera streams, I don't have any way of knowing the computer addresses for them."

George and Marley nodded at the screen, they didn't have a clue what a 'computer address' was.

"You're looking blank. Computer address is an Internet Protocol address," Sam explained. They stared back even blanker. "It's like a house address for the Internet. It links all the computers in the world together through the numbers. Without that, it's impossible to find the camera's video stream. It would be like trying to find a house in a street without knowing the address, street or town. So I must have the codes from your headmistress's office, once I have those I can set a divert and get them recorded for you. Meanwhile, I've nearly finished the app development for the phone, that was easy. But I'll need the phone for an hour, I think, to get it loaded and tested."

"Are......are you saying that we need to somehow get into Mrs T office and steal the codes?" Marley's voice trembled, his bottom lip quivering.

"Yep, that's exactly right," Sam said, not looking up while she tapped at speed on the keyboard. It didn't seem a problem to her.

George and Marley thought about the implications in silence.

"You mean we need to get the log-in details from Mrs Tinsley's office!" Marley repeated in a blind panic. "That's impossible." Marley jumped up, pacing around the room.

"Not impossible," said Sam. "Just not easy."

"We can't do that." Marley turned to George, terror struck. "How can we do that? You have to agree it's insane."

Sam jabbed at the keyboard again.

"The codes will be in the large cabinet Mrs T keeps on the far side of her office. When I've been in there, I noticed one of the drawers has COUNCIL written on it in big letters. If we can get into there I think we will find them," said George.

"Great," replied Sam still not looking up, as if breaking into your head teacher's office was the most natural thing in the world. "Just bring them to me this weekend with the phone as we agreed. Got to go boys, this code won't write itself." With a wink, the screen died. Marley studied the screen misty-eyed for a moment.

"So what do we do now?" Marley asked, his shoulders deflating.

"We'll have to get the codes from Mrs T's office. It's as simple as that." George replied, trying to convince himself.

"That's just it, it isn't simple, is it? We haven't time. It means we have to do it in the next two days! And we need to get hold of your Dad's phone, like now." Marley stared at the wall.

"Come on. We can find a way. Let's try to put a plan together." George picked up a pen and paper from the desk and turned to Marley.

"Time to put together..." he paused for effect, "...Operation 'Let's Get The Codes From Mrs Tinsley's Office'".

Marley sighed.

15 TIME FOR AN OPERATION

On Friday morning George and Marley approached the school gates searching for signs of Mrs T and Clive. Clive would have to be dealt with for their grand strategy to work. They'd made a plan yesterday evening, today was their last chance to collect the codes - it was now or never.

Mrs T loved to bring Clive into work. He could be found in the corner of her office occasionally rising from his basket to diligently inspect the playground. He couldn't venture out much as the children adored him, and he'd be mobbed like a superstar if he ever left the office. He sometimes went to relieve himself, but this was under the watchful eye of his minder Mrs T.

Marley was more concerned about Pickled Daniels, as there was always a chance she would be there *accidentally* tripping up year ones as they arrived and it freaked him out.

Mrs T pulled into the school car park.

"Look," said Marley nudging George, "I can see Clive's head in the passenger seat." Sure enough, there was Clive, wet tongue dangling from the passenger window.

George spotted Pickled Daniels and jabbed Marley. She held a large, black bin bag and a grab stick shaped like a monstrous hand, picking rubbish. The playground was full of children darting around and playing games. Some parents were chatting while other children zipped past. Pickled Daniels worked slowly, collecting debris around the edge of the playground.

Usually George and Marley would have joined in the games, and Pickled Daniels would have melted into the background. But this morning they both watched her rather like two vigilant bird spotters with eye strain. She was a good twenty metres from them, oblivious to anyone watching.

Then she did it. She gripped an old crisp packet, deposited it into her black bag, then turned to a small group of parents, huddled in conversation. Their packed lunch boxes and games kits were strewn over the dirt. A drawstring was slightly undone, and even Marley from some distance could see the black shorts protruding over the top.

Pickled Daniels whipped around, dipped her grab stick into the edge of the bag, made contact with the shorts, clamping the plastic mechanical hand. In an instant, they dropped into her black bin liner. The whole process took less than a second, and no one had noticed. Pickled Daniels moved over to a sweet wrapper and carried on as if nothing happened, whistling to herself.

"Did you see that?" said Marley turning to George with a look of utter frustration on his face. "What do we do?"

"We can't do anything today." George sighed. "We need everything to be as normal as possible. Just pretend we haven't seen it."

Marley was fuming.

Mrs T came sweeping through the playground with little Clive running excitedly at her heel. Children mobbed him, he didn't break step. It was like he had trained at a top military dog academy, not breaking rank for a second. In fact, Clive had body image issues as he really thought he was the headmaster, not a small Chihuahua, so kept his head raised running proudly next to Mrs T. In his mind, he was the one leading the way!

The first lesson seemed to drag on forever. George and Marley couldn't concentrate, their eyes kept straying to the giant clock above the whiteboard. Eventually, the minutes ticked by and the bell signalled the start of the mid-morning break. The class erupted into a cacophony of noise as the mass rushed to the door before heading to the playground.

"OK," said George. "We have twenty minutes. Let's do it." He picked up his football and headed for the door.

OPERATION "LET'S GET THE CODES FROM MRS TINSLEY'S OFFICE"

Timing was critical, but so was a little luck. They needed Mr Savage out of the classroom within two minutes of break starting, or they had no chance of completing the whole plan in time. While everyone rushed around the playground in a frenzy, they hung close to the classroom window. Mr Savage picked up some papers. He paused to read something from a book.

"What's he doing?" said Marley, looking at his watch. "We need him out of there within the next minute. He normally goes straight to the staff room after class." They kicked a ball, glancing through the window every now and then. Mr Savage did a sweep of the room whistling to himself. Then, with a final rub of the whiteboard, made for the exit, closing the door behind him.

"Right. That's it, time to go. Go, Marley...go now." George pushed him in the back.

Marley was off. George doggedly scanned the playground for any inquisitive playground monitors. Marley was in. He inched opened the door taking a tiny peep around the edge. All clear.

Marley slipped through, breathing heavily - a gleam of sweat on his brow. Like an army commando, he ducked down, crawling under the window. If he were seen in the classroom one of the children would tell a monitor, who would inform Mrs Walker, who would blag to Mrs Tinsley. It didn't bear thinking about. Marley shuddered. He continued his slow ninja wriggle.

Craning his neck, he peered up at the display. There it was, the object he needed, in all its beautiful glory. Propped up as part of a large dinosaur display was a replica bone from a Brontosaurus. The local museum had left the bone for the school to display for their annual open evening. The replica appeared wholly real, like a fresh bone which could have really come from any animal, except for the size of it. It was massive. Really massive.

Marley heard voices in the corridor. He froze,

pressing himself against the wall, willing himself smaller. He waited, his heart beating in his ears.

Finally, the voices drifted away. Reaching across the table, careful not to disturb anything else, Marley lifted the gigantic bone. It was nearly as long as his arm and much more cumbersome than he was expecting.

He dropped to the floor again, dragging the monstrosity behind. Finally, he prised open the door.

"Come on. We've only sixteen minutes left."

The operation was now in its critical stage. George and Marley strolled around the edge of the playground trying to look nonchalant while carrying an ancient, colossal dinosaur bone - which isn't easy.

"OK," said George rather like a sergeant major, "staffroom coming up on our left. I'm going to glance in quickly as we walk past. Act normal. Keep the bone hidden."

As they passed the staffroom, Marley could feel the bone digging into his hip. They reached the edge of the playground in front of Mrs Tinsley's office. Fewer children played at this end.

"I need to get this bone out," complained Marley as the sun burned down from a cloudless sky. "It's too hot to have a large dinosaur bone in your pants."

George glanced at his watch. Time was ticking by.

"We've already used six minutes, only fourteen left. We need to hurry up," George said. "Can you see Clive?"

They both peered at Mrs Tinsley's office, and there was Clive, perched on a shelf, standing up on his hind legs looking longingly out of the window at the freedom of the playground.

"Look," said Marley pointing at the office," Mrs T's left the window open for Clive."

Clive was harmless but had a tremendous bark (well yap would be a better description) on him, so they had to distract him.

"OK. I make it ten thirty-seven and twenty seconds," said George pulling Marley into a huddle.

"Yer, mine's about eight seconds different."

"Right, we have to do this now," said George. "I'm going, and you need to be ready in another two minutes and thirty seconds exactly."

He left Marley standing alone at the edge of the playground. Marley shivered, this final part of the plan had to go right!

16 CLIVE LOVES A BIG BONE

This was the hardest, most daring part of the plan. If they got caught, they'd be in serious trouble. Breaking into your headmistress's office is plain madness! George had to get through reception and into Mrs Tinsley's room. Children weren't generally seen around the front of the school during break and George would be leaving the school playground which was not permitted at all. George stood subconsciously pulling his body in, trying to shrink, of course, this was ridiculous.

Glancing at his watch he shifted his weight onto his other leg, poking his head around the corner of the building. He spied the front reception door ten metres away. The coast was clear. He sauntered nonchalantly, coming in line with the front office. Glancing in, he noticed that no one was in it. What a lucky break!

He squeezed through the front door. Crouching on the floor, George panted and stayed where he was for a second or two getting his breath back. He had one minute and thirty seconds left.

Marley looked at his watch and moved closer to the window. Time to act. Drawing the humungous bone from his trousers he used his body to mask it. Eventually, the colossal bone was entirely noticeable to Clive who was perched in the window, a befuddled look on his face.

Clive had his mind on food. It is a known fact (probably) that ninety-eight percent of the time dogs are either thinking or dreaming about food, with Clive it was ninety-nine, point nine, nine, nine percent. Then it appeared before him, as if in a beautiful daydream - like a magical apparition. The most substantial bone he had ever seen. An edible bone of majestic beauty. He had to have it. He panted with longing, licking his chops.

"Clive," whispered Marley. "Come on Clive, through the window." Marley pointed at the open window as if it would help. Five seconds to go. Now Clive wasn't exceptionally bright, in fact, one might think of him as slightly thick. But even Clive couldn't turn down the most prominent bone he had ever seen. Luckily the two pieces of information came together in his brain within the next three hundred milliseconds - window and bone. And with two seconds to spare Clive made a jump for it. In one glorious instant, he was flying through the air with his mind fixed on the food in front of him. Tongue flapping out of the side of his mouth as he careered towards Marley and the alluring bone.

Outside the door, George watched the countdown. Three, two, one. Pushing down on the handle he gently moved the door, easing himself through the gap into Mrs T's office.

He was in. Clive was gone. George shook, his face turning grey; if he were caught stealing in the headmistress's office his life would be hell. He'd be on a computer games and phone ban for a year and undoubtedly be thrown out of school.

Outside the window, he could see Marley stroking Clive who was trying to gnaw on the dinosaur bone. He didn't have long. Quivering, he inspected the room. To the untrained eye, you would be mistaken for thinking Mrs T was related to the Royal family, her entire office was covered with royal wedding memorabilia, from gaudy ancient mugs to commemoration plates hung on the walls.

George sneaked over to the filing cabinets. Over the last week George had deliberately gone to see Mrs T about any issues he could think of, so he had been in the room at least four times to work out where everything was kept. On a couple of occasions working his way around the oak desk while talking to Mrs Tinsley, peering into the filing cabinets when they were open. 'Council Communication' was in the second drawer down in the left unit. Standing next to the cabinet now, with palms sweating, he pulled the drawer. It wouldn't budge. He tried again. Nothing. Finally, yanking as hard as he could. Two royal mugs toppled, rolled to one side and then fell. George reacted quickly, jumping to one side and rather like a world cup goalkeeper dived forward catching them in two hands.

Calming himself with deep breaths, he carefully placed them back on the cabinet. He pulled a second time. Now the drawer creakily moved, thankfully sliding out to reveal the contents neatly labelled in folders. George sighed. Sweating, he thumbed through each heading, finding 'Council Communication' on the fifth folder. George pulled it out and shakily lay it on the top of the cabinet. He didn't understand most of it. Sam had told him it was "CCTV" that he needed. Finally, George discovered it, a label protruding which read 'County Council Remote CCTV Monitoring', below were lots of complicated paragraphs of explanation and right at the bottom was a web address and password for the school. Exactly what he needed. George beamed. He stuffed the page into his pocket and snapped the folder shut before returning it to the cabinet.

Now he had what he wanted everything came into focus again, he could hear the sounds from the playground. Time to get out! Opening the office door a little, he peered into the corridor. No one. Slipping out he approached reception. Just as he was about to clear the main door he heard a voice. He froze.

"What you doin?" George recognised the voice immediately. He turned around.

"Erm. Nothing," gulped George, facing Pickled Daniels. She was holding a bucket and mop in her hands.

"It's nothing, Mrs Daniels, to you." She pointed her mop at him like a soldier's bayonet.

"S...SSSS...SS...Sorry, Mrs Daniels. It's nothing, Mrs Daniels." George was trembling.

Pickled Daniels meandered up close to him, an offensive odour hit George. He couldn't move. She took another slow step towards him, their noses were almost touching now. George could feel her wheezing.

"You're not allowed in here during break," she said very slowly, spraying spit as she talked.

She had black hair sprouting from her chin, a broad frown on her shrivelled forehead.

"Eh...I was just making sure that my games kit was all there, I was worried that my mum had left out my shorts."

"Why have you come through the front of the school though? Children aren't allowed around here. Are you following me?" Pickled Daniels was enjoying herself, she didn't usually get a chance to tell children off.

George twisted and squirmed. "Sorry, Mrs Daniels, I wasn't thinking. Of course, I should have gone through the classroom. Of course, I'm not following you." George stood a little taller.

Pickled Daniels didn't know how to continue, she wasn't used to doing this. Her eyes bored into George.

"Well, I'm watching you kid. And your snotty friend. Now.....now get out!"

Pickled Daniels pointed the way with her damp mop.

George didn't need to be told twice. He sprinted through reception, stumbling into the door in his haste to open it. George was out.

Marley had problems. Clive was so pleased with the bone he just wouldn't let go. Marley held the bone right off the ground with Clive dangling from it. His teeth sunk into the bone flesh, holding on for dear life. Marley was shaking it a little, but that just made Clive swing about in the wind, more determined than ever to hang on.

"What you doing?" George asked. "We've only got six minutes left."

"I can't do anything with him. I think he winded himself a little when he jumped out of the window, when he opened his eyes he just grabbed onto the bone, and he's been like this ever since. I'm not sure if he can even breathe properly. Is he dead?"

George inspected Clive. Clive's tiny eyes followed him as he moved his head, so George knew he was all right. He gave Clive a little poke. Nothing.

"On the plus side," added Marley, smiling. "He's been as quiet as a mouse. Well, like a mouse with a mouth crammed full of bone."

"Well we've got to get him back into Mrs T's office, so we have got to get him off. I'll try tickling him while you shake the bone."

Clive whimpered a little but clung frantically to the bone. George tried some more aggressive tickling, Clive kicked his dinky feet. Suddenly Clive released, tumbling to the ground. Immediately he started yapping.

"Clive...sush......Quick, hide the bone again! Everyone's going to look over," George said. Sure enough, some of the younger children heard Clive and were heading over.

"I've an idea! We'll have to pretend Clive's escaped."

"But he's not letting me go." Marley ran in little circles with Clive chasing, eyes rolling. George acted fast. He plucked Clive up, dumping him in the arms of a year two boy.

"Clive's escaped from Mrs Tinsley office. Go and tell Mrs Walker." As they got further away, they could still hear Clive barking in the distance. Clive loved that bone.

George glanced at Marley. They'd done it. They had the codes. Now they just had the simple task of depositing a gigantic dinosaur bone back to the classroom!

17 ERNIE'S BOX OF MAGIC

It was Saturday afternoon, the day after the successful completion of 'Operation Code' and George was in the front room with his mum.

"What is he doing in there?" George's mum asked. She'd been spying out of the living room window watching Uncle Ernie struggle with bits of wood carrying them from the car to the garage.

"He made your father go all over town," she continued, sipping a cup of tea.

George looked up from his homework. "He's making me a magic box for the talent show."

"Does he know what he's doing?"

"I think so, he said he once worked with a magician years and years ago. I can't do the show without it."

George's dad helped Ernie get the last items out of the car and closed the boot.

"Well, I just hope he tidies up. It's hard enough looking after you and Phoebe. Oh, and by the way. I'm doing a big shop later, can you come with me, I need help with the bags."

George jumped up. "What?" George

shouted. "I can't, I've got to go and see Sam with Marley."

"You can play your computer games anytime. I need help, no one does anything around this house."

"I....I...I've got to go to Sam's. It's really important."

"Really important? I don't think playing computer games with your cousin is really important, is it? I need help around the house. You're coming with me young man, and that's the end of it." She slammed the dishwasher door shut.

George gave the kitchen door a little kick. He slipped out to the garage. Dad was arranging wood.

"Is that OK Ernie?" Dad shouted at Ernie.

"Sorry, didn't catch that." Ernie cupped a hand to his ear.

"IS THAT EVERYTHING?"

"Oh. I think so lad." Ernie surveyed the area. He'd transformed the garage into a makeshift carpenter's workshop. Tools and wood dust lay everywhere. Resting to one side was the half-finished box. A piece of real beauty. It looked to be fashioned from a single block of pure oak rather than been bashed together in a garage by an octogenarian with gas problems. It had intricate, smooth corners with hand-carved doves coming out of the edges and the base tapered off with a small bead around the edge. George could see the glass and mirrors carefully set at angles, neatly glued in.

"Did you really make this Uncle Ernie?" George was stunned. He ran his hands around the edge of the box.

"Yes, it's quite something isn't it," said George's dad coming over. "You didn't know that Ernie was an amateur carpenter, or should I say, craftsman, did you, George?"

"Does it work yet?" George was getting excited.

"Not quite finished yet boy." Ernie smiled. "But I can show you a little of how it works. Pass me that small tin of paint there, and I can pretend that's your raw cake. Then this one can be your cooked one." He presented a small tin of black paint. Ernie carefully placed the tin into the centre of the box and then got hold of the other one.

"Right, you two stand over there." Ernie let out a little fart.

"Quite exciting really, isn't it George?" Dad said pinching his nose.

"First you need to tell your audience what you are doing. Say this is the cake and all that about how you can make it bake quickly. You know what to say, lad. So you place it in the box here at the top. So you can see that it is there, yes?"

They both nodded, enthralled by Ernie's demonstration. Ernie was wheezing a little now.

"Right, now distract your audience. On the back of the box is a small lever covered by this little panel. If you slide the panel back then press the handle, the mirrors spring to a different position. Like this." The paint pot transformed from the original black one to the new red one.

"Wow," George said excitedly. "That's amazing. It's magically turned into the other pot."

"Yes lad, that's the idea. But the black one's still there you see." Beaming, he picked up the black one to show them. "It's just hidden by the mirrors. The best thing to do at the end is walk off with the box. Otherwise, someone might see inside it. If you want to reset it just pull the lever back until it clicks into position."

George's dad clapped.

"Uncle Ernie, that's excellent," he said.

"When do you think you'll be finished?"

Ernie rubbed his forehead as he thought about it.

"Give me a few more days lad. Got to varnish it yet."

"Thanks, Uncle Ernie."

George sprinted to his room. He fired up his computer, tapping his toes waiting for the thing to work. Sam's beaming face appeared on the screen.

"Hey George, how are you? When are you coming over today?" Sam asked. Her headphones were draped around her neck, she looked very relaxed.

"That's why I'm calling. I can't come over this weekend." Sam stopped typing and stared at the screen.

"But I need the codes and the phone George. It's only one week to the show. When can you get them to me?" It was the first time George had seen Sam agitated.

"Yer, I'm sorry. The only time I can come over is Thursday evening, mum and dad are out then."

"Thursday! But that only leaves two days till the show." Sam replied her face in a scowl.

"I know, sorry Sam. Can you do it in two days?"

There was a pause as Sam thought it over.

"I don't know George. I don't think I can," said Sam dejectedly now scribbling some notes with a pen.

"You've got to try Sam. Please, it's our only chance," pleaded George. Sam paced the room. Eventually, she spoke.

"OK....erm....I'll try. But I can't guarantee anything. Let's meet Thursday."

"OK, thanks, Sam....and sorry again...I'd better go. See you then," said George. He pressed the icon, and the screen went blank.

George sat with his face in his hands gazing out his bedroom window. Perhaps that mean old lady Pickled Daniels couldn't be caught after all. Their plans were all falling apart.

18 FIRE, FIRE MY PANTS ARE ON FIRE!

It was Tuesday evening, Baking Club had just begun. Pickled Daniels rummaged through piles of junk in her cleaning cupboard. The club had to be killed off once and for all. She delved into the back, pushing around clear boxes of fluid and accumulated clutter.

"Yous must be here. Come on treacle toes. Show mummy where you are. Come out, come out, wherever you are. Where are you my beautiful white sticks of light," she sang quietly to herself. She sifted through more junk and was now in the far cobwebby corner of the cupboard. Finally, her hand settled on an ancient box of candles.

"Good girls, mummy needs you for a minute."

Retreating she grabbed the rickety old step-ladder. The smell of coconut and honey drifted in the air. The excited voices of children filled the school, she tutted. The happiness made her ill.

In Class 3A she stopped to open her shawl, beads of sweat ran down her brow from hauling the step ladder, she whipped out a small bottle of rum and had a quick lug. Gaining in confidence, she bent down and grabbed the first candle she could lay her hands on. Digging into her pockets, she located a box of matches. Hands shaking she attempted to light the candle, as she brought the wobbling match up it went out.

"Don't be so naughty for mummy now. Mummy knows best."

Feeling dizzy, she fumbled in the pack extracting another which burst into life as she struck it. This time the candle lit. Holding the burning candle in her left hand, she slowly climbed the rickety step-ladder. She wafted it above her head. In the corner of the room was the smoke alarm, that was what she was after.

Gingerly stepping onto the second rung of the ladder she passed the candle between hands presenting it higher in the air, if anyone had come in at that point they would have thought she looked like a very filthy and rather decrepit version of the Statue of Liberty. In a sense that's how Pickled Daniels felt, she wanted her school for herself, she wanted liberty from the children.

The ladder wobbled. Pickled Daniels lost grip and the candle went hurtling to the floor landing next to the hamster cage in a bundle of loose bedding. The paper lit. Small flames rose up around her, and black smoke billowed from the little fire.

"Aaahhhhhhhhhhhhhhhh……"

Pickled Daniels let out a panicked scream, nearly losing her balance. Fire licked at the small fan heater. It wouldn't be long before the whole classroom went up. She focused frantically around the room, wondering what to do. Flames had now caught hold of the hamster food container, causing even darker smoke to billow out.

"Right, I'ms coming to get you."

Launching herself from the ladder, she hurtled through the air landing directly onto the mass of flames. It was probably the furthest she'd jumped in fifty years.

"Oh...ah..ah....oh...." she cried stamping her feet. The fire alarm burst into life, ringers going berserk in every room of the school.

In baking club, Mrs Walker was demonstrating the art of getting air into a cake with ten eager faces watching her every move. The alarm pierced the lesson. Mrs Walker flipped into authority mode. Dusting her hands over the bowl, she barked out some orders.

"OK. The fire alarm is going off. Please slowly put down all your cooking equipment and assemble in a line by the door." Marley glanced nervously at George, another odd thing going on in the school.

Pickled Daniels had finally got the situation under control. She stamped her mouldy feet on the small fire until it eventually snuffed out, stuffed the spent candle down her top and started wafting her shawl to remove the smoky mist hanging in the air. But her panic was notching up a level. She had a large candle stuffed in her bra, a box of matches and a ladder. It didn't look right – you wouldn't need to be a police detective to work out she was up to no good. She grabbed the matches stuffing them down the other side of her bra.

Mrs T had been in her office when the alarm went off, she was born for these sort of situations, you don't become headmistress without having some yearning for power and control. She marched down the corridor, head held high. She knew the fire brigade would be on their way.

Pickled Daniels pulled at the step-ladder frantically searching, trembling now with the nerves brewing in her stomach - she had to hide it. In the corner was Mr Savage's cupboard where he kept his scientific equipment for class experiments. Pickled Daniels quickly rammed it in, closing the door behind, it would have to do. She poked her grimy head into the corridor. Mrs T marched around the corner, their eyes met.

"Mrs Daniels, are you OK? The alarm has been going off, you should be out of the school," shouted Mrs T concerned. She broke into a jog. Pickled Daniels opened the door a little more. Smoke billowed into the corridor.

"I knows but I was worried about the children you see," Pickled Daniels replied trying to put on her very concerned voice. "I was checking this room and discovered the fire. I had to put it out."

Mrs T pushed open the door and saw the remnants of the small fire. Beaming now she snapped her head back to Pickled Daniels.

"That's very noble of you Mrs Daniels, thank you for doing that. I am very impressed. But what have I always said about safety first? You should not put yourself in danger, leave it for the professionals to deal with." She smiled. "But you may have just saved some lives tonight. We must go now."

Pickled Daniels wobbled after her. Unfortunately, the candle was tangled in her dirty clothing and jabbed into her body at a bizarre angle. To make matters worse, the smouldering tip was in direct contact with her skin.

"Are you OK? You seem to be walking a little awkwardly. Did you injure yourself putting out the fire?"

"I might have done yes, you sees I needed to act quickly. I just happened to be passing the room just when the alarm went off and saw a little smoke. My only thought was not for me own safety, but that of the children." Pickled Daniels smiled to herself, this had all worked out very well.

"That's very commendable," said Mrs T proudly.

Outside, baking club had assembled in a small huddle on the playing field. Mrs Walker had a register in hand ticking off names.

George felt slightly put out by the alarm, his cakes promised to be the best he'd ever done, and now they would be ruined. Everyone was chatting about the alarm. Of course, no one believed it was the real thing, no one ever does. Marley spied

Pickled Daniels and diverted his stare.

"Is everyone accounted for Mrs Walker?" Mrs T asked.

"Yes, with yourself and Mrs Daniels that's everyone who was in the school."

Pickled Daniels hung around behind Mrs T desperately readjusting her clothing to stop the candle causing irreparable damage.

Then came the wailing of distance bells. Ten seconds later the fire engine appeared. Firefighters piled out, and two of them rushed towards the entrance, dressed ready for the worst. The fireman in charge jumped out of the enormous engine and jogged over to the school group. He was nearly as massive as the appliance.

"Chief Fire Officer O'Gorman, that's O, G, O, R, M, A, N. Is the headmaster around?" He barked, booming at anyone who would listen, eyes darting furiously.

"Yes, I'm the **headmistress**, Mrs Tinsley."

"Oh. Right love. OK. You're in charge, are you? Anyone missing?" O'Gorman replied as if bellowing out orders to a minion.

"No all accounted for, and you'll find the fire has been put out in classroom three A. Mrs Daniels here is the hero of the hour. She found the fire and without any thought for herself dealt with it admirably." Mrs T announced flamboyantly to the fire chief. Putting a hand out as if to present Pickled Daniels to the world.

"Very good. Well, let's see what we find. We have to investigate every fire anyway to find the cause. Have you any idea what caused it, Mrs Daniels?"

Pickled Daniels looked at her shoes, refusing to meet O'Gorman's eye. *I have to say something* she thought, almost mesmerised. Having a wax candle shoved into her belly button was very, very distracting. Now everyone was staring at Pickled Daniels, as if she were about to spill an exciting revelation. The blood rushed into her cheeks. An idea struck! She remembered that when she dropped the candle, it was next to a small portable fan.

"Wells. I can't says for sure but me thinks there was a small fan, like a portable electrical thing around the fire. That was part of it." Pickled Daniels felt relieved she had come up with something.

"Electrical fault ay, very good. OK, well that is something for my men to look into. Right. Stay here until we give you the all clear." He marched off, his gigantic boots stomping on the grass.

"Mrs Daniels, I think you ought to go home,

you look dreadful. It's been a long day, and I can deal with the fire brigade from here. Let's do the cleaning in the morning instead, and baking club will be cancelled now anyway." said Mrs T.

"Yes, me thinks I will." Pickled Daniels was exhausted, though happier than she'd been for a long time. It was precisely the result she had been hoping for. She hobbled slowly towards her bungalow with a great big smile on her face.

19 THE LINE DANCING KING AND QUEEN

George's parents had one real passion in life. It was a passion that you probably wouldn't be able to guess if you saw them in the street: American line dancing. It was actually more an obsession than a passion. George's mum had started over twenty years ago and then dragged his dad along. Ever since they'd spent Thursday evenings in a local hall dancing their hearts out. Over those twenty years, she'd become very accomplished, and George's mum spent hours devising new routines and moves, they even dressed up in jeans, cowboy boots and checked shirts. Of course, George was mortified by the whole embarrassing thing, but it did mean that George could track his dad's movements, which is exactly what he needed to get his mitts on his smartphone.

Marley and George had planned to meet at seven-thirty, as George's mum and dad were due to be at line dancing by eight. At seven-twenty the doorbell went.

"I'll get it," George shouted, running for the door. Marley was soaked to the skin, it was pouring with rain. He came in shaking his hair like a wet dog.

"Is everything ready?" Marley whispered. George peered up the stairs to check no one was listening.

"Yer, they'll be getting ready to go soon. Did you bring your bike?"

"I've got it, but the chain fell off in College Road, I had to stop and put it back on. I couldn't do it very well." He held out his hands to show they were covered in grease. In the kitchen, George poured milk from the fridge. Marley washed his hands.

"Where is it then?" whispered Marley, finishing at the sink.

"I haven't got it yet." Marley's face dropped.

They heard the sounds of feet padding down the stairs. George's dad tramped into the kitchen without a shirt on.

"Have you seen my denim shirt with the grey pearls on it?" George's dad shouted up the stairs as he whirled around the kitchen. "Has it been ironed?" He scrabbled through the dry clothes in the washing basket.

George's mother came down the stairs

shouting, "Have you looked in your cupboard?"

George found it funny when his mum spoke to his dad like he was another child. It happened a lot.

"I've looked there. And where's my wallet and phone? I can't find them either."

"I don't know," snapped George's mother. It was like two gladiators fighting with words instead of weapons. George and Marley sat grinning, listening to the whole exchange.

"I can never find anything in this house," George's dad muttered.

"We've got to go," mum shouted.

The doorbell went again.

"Oh Goodness," George said. "I'd forgotten about Jennie."

"Jennie? The babysitter? How can we get out with her here?" said Marley.

"She's not very bright, Marley, leave her to me," said George.

Jennie stood at the door dripping, holding a paper bag crammed full of sweets, chews and chocolate bars, and in her other hand - two litres of fizzy pop.

"Why are you so wet Jennie, is your brolly not working?" asked George's mum.

Jennie thought for a moment. The cogs in

her brain turned exceptionally slowly.

"Oh. I forgot my brolly," she eventually replied.

"Well, let's get you dried off and make you a cup of tea," said George's mum smiling, hustling her into the kitchen.

"Hello George," said Jennie in her monotone voice.

"Hi, Jennie." George raised his hand a little.

Jennie's arrival was the call to action George and Marley needed. They had to steal the phone before mum and dad left for the evening.

Jennie plonked herself down in front of the TV. Pulling out a bag of sweets she reached for the remote. Uncle Ernie was sat in the comfy chair at the other end of the living room, snoring loudly.

"You get yourself settled then, Jennie," George's mum said. "So Phoebe is upstairs in her pyjamas reading, and George has his friend Marley over for an hour or so. Oh, and Ernie's asleep."

"Uh, hu," replied Jennie not taking her eyes off the screen and dipping her plump hand into the bag of sweets.

Jennie flicked through the channels, her mouth full of Haribo, happy as a chimpanzee with a fruit salad.

George's mum made for the stairs. "Are you ready? We need to go," she screamed.

George and Marley waited for mum to reach the top step.

"Right, Dad's phone will probably be in his

coat pocket, he always leaves it there. Cover me."
George crept into the hallway and approached
the coat rack. Marley wasn't quite sure what *'cover
me'* meant, so he took it to mean 'watch me'.
George patted each coat pocket. It was hard to
concentrate, not only was there the sound of his
parents shouting at each other from their
bedroom, Jennie had the TV turned up so loudly
the theme tune for Coronation Street was blasting
all over the house.

"It's got to be here somewhere," George lay
the wax jacket on the floor. Opening each pocket,
in turn, he pushed his hand deep inside.

"Come on George, hurry up," Marley
scanned the stairs, concerned that George's
parents might appear at any moment.

But it wasn't his parents who appeared at the
top of the stairs. It was Phoebe!

"What you doing?" Phoebe
shouted at the top of her voice watching George
frisk the coats.

"Phoebe, be quiet." George held a finger to
his mouth.

"Why?" Phoebe asked, still shouting.

"Shhh," added Marley, waving his hands for
her to quieten down.

"Why have you got Dad's coat?" screamed Phoebe.

"Marley, go and talk to her," said George desperately waving Marley towards the bottom of the stairs. His facing reddening.

"Why me?"

"Cause you're meant to be covering me," said George as if the statement was reason enough. George gave up on the wax jacket and swapped it for Dad's work coat. Marley stepped up a couple of the lower steps. Phoebe was glued to the landing holding her Humphrey toy in one hand and sucking her other thumb. She was too old to be sucking a thumb but had never really grown out of the habit.

"Phoebe, go back to your room," said Marley in a muted whisper.

"Why?" It was Phoebe's favourite question.

"Shhh," replied Marley. They could hear Jennie rustling in her sweet bag in the other room, and there were some mumbled sounds from the parent's room.

"We're just looking for something. How's Humphrey?" Marley desperately tried to distract her. George was getting towards the end of the third coat. Finally, he connected with a phone.

Grabbing it, his heart raced. He whisked out the phone slipping it into his own pocket.

"I've got it," he whispered to Marley. Marley grinned.

"What have you got?" shouted

Phoebe, tramping down the stairs. George gathered up the coats and attempted to put them back on the hangers in some kind of order. George's dad dashed out of his room dressed in a denim shirt and jeans, he was threading a belt through his jeans as he hurried down the stairs, catching up with Phoebe.

"What have you got?" she repeated as she reached the bottom of the stairs.

George and Marley froze in terror and peered at Dad, looking like a couple of large-eyed meerkats.

"What are you two up to?" he asked, smiling at them. He walked straight past to the hall table, peering around for his wallet and phone. George's shoulders relaxed a little, but he had to get Phoebe off the scent.

"Jennie dropped some of her sweets, we were just looking for them for her," said George.

"Can I have some?" Phoebe replied holding out her hand. Dad wasn't paying much attention as he was too busy with his own problems.

"Have you seen my wallet and phone?" he screamed again to his wife. George and Marley took that as a signal, escaping to the kitchen. Phoebe followed.

George's mum rushed down the stairs pushing an earring in as she went.

"We're going to be late." She hastily reviewed the kitchen collecting her handbag from the back of a chair. She could see her husband standing around not really doing anything, much like a lemon.

"Goodness, you're useless. Don't just stand there, we've got to go."

She produced two pairs of cowboy boots.

"Well I can't find my phone, I've got my wallet, but no phone," George's dad confirmed, pushing on his boots.

"You don't need your phone anyway, we'll be dancing the whole time. Guys, have any of you seen your dad's phone?" she called. George, Marley and Phoebe were standing in the kitchen doorway looking at them.

I just have to lie, thought George. It was a dilemma, but he had no choice. It was for the greater good.

"No, haven't seen it anywhere," George said, passing a quick glance at Marley.

"No mummy," replied Phoebe.

"OK, got to go. Bye kids, not to bed too late." George's mum bustled out, trailed by dad.

"Bye kids, see you later. Bye Jennie," said Dad.

There was a muffled reply from the living room. But to be fair, it is hard to talk with seventeen Maltesers in your mouth.

20 JENNIE'S NOT A PROPER BABYSITTER

"Your Dad would go loopy if he realised we had this," Marley said admiring the very latest in phone technology.

"Yer, I know. We've got to be careful with it." George replied, taking a couple of custard creams from the biscuit tin. He handed the tin to Marley.

"We need to be at Sam's in fifteen minutes, we'd better get going."

"What about Jennie?"

"Don't worry about Jennie," said George munching on his third biscuit. "Watch this."

Uncle Ernie was still asleep even though the sound coming from the TV was louder than a jet fighter taking off.

"Jennie, we're just going skydiving with a shark, is that alright?" George said to the back of Jennie's head.

"Uh, huh," replied Jennie. Her body didn't move a muscle.

"OK, then we thought we would go and see a

vampire, is that OK?" continued George. Marley giggled.

"Uh, huh," Jennie agreed and pushed her hand into the sweet bag, eyes fixed on the TV. Uncle Ernie joined in the conversation with a small fart, he adjusted his head a little and continued snoring. Jennie seemed oblivious to it. This just made Marley laugh more.

"How does your uncle sleep through that?" stated Marley.

"He's old," replied George. "He seems to be asleep most of the time. You see, she's not much of a babysitter. I think mum gets her to look after Ernie rather than us anyway."

"Have you got the codes?" stated Marley.

"Oh, goodness. No, I nearly forget them, that would have been terrible, they're in my room."

George darted upstairs. Ballet music drifted from Phoebe's room, she was apparently practising for the show again.

"Got them, let's go," said George, waving a piece of paper.

George and Marley quietly slipped out of the back door, grabbing their bikes for the trip across town.

George slowed down as they got to Sam's

street, letting Marley catch up.

"Come on, we haven't got long," George said dumping their bikes. Marley was suddenly conscious of how he looked. Licking his hand, he smoothed down his hair as George rang the doorbell.

Eventually, they heard Sam running down the stairs, she whipped open the door.

"Watcha boys, come in." Marley was entranced, just seeing her for half a second had thrown him. He was absolutely convinced he was in love.

Sam was already furiously typing on the keyboard when they reached her room. Lines of computer code whizzed across the monitors.

"Why didn't you come on Saturday. We've only got tomorrow before the show."

"Sorry, Sam. My mum wouldn't let me go out Saturday and then on Sunday we had to go and visit Gran."

"Well luckily I think I'm nearly there now, should just be a case of getting this onto the phone and let's see what we've got. Let's just hope it works."

"Here's the phone, Sam," George said, carefully removing it from his jacket. He placed it on the desk, unwrapping it like lost treasure.

"OK, let's have a look." Sam pressed the touch screen, it burst into life.

"Yer, we can do something with this. Latest generation apps will go onto this OK. He has security set up, so I need a pin number or a fingerprint. I take it you haven't brought his finger with you?" Sam said laughing to herself.

"Errr...no," George said, nervously. "Do we need it?"

"I'm only joshing with you George, I can get around that." Sam opened one of the drawers next to her desk and rummaged through a mass of cables. Marley sighed, his eyes glossing over with love.

"This is what we need." She finished pulling one black cable, plugging the phone in. Sam was away again, tapping on the keyboard like a nervous Irish dancer.

"So, all we need to do now is hack into the phone, dump the app onto it and then get it to link to the school cameras and record. A piece of cake. Have you got the codes?"

George and Marley were a bit bewildered but nodded their heads as Sam continued to type and talk. George delved into his back pocket retrieving the paper with the codes on it.

"Give me ten minutes will you?" She

continued typing in silence. Again, they just nodded their heads, understanding little of what she was saying. George and Marley sat perched on the bed like a pair of befuddled bats waiting for dusk.

"We haven't got long Sam, mum and dad are out line dancing, the babysitter doesn't know we're gone," said George looking at his watch. "If Jennie's sweets run out she'll go to the biscuit tin in the kitchen. She might notice we're missing, or Phoebe might notice and raise the alarm!" He had a look of real concern on his face.

Sam wasn't listening, switching her attention between the three giant screens in front of her she drummed furiously on the keyboard. The council website appeared on the screen, and she entered the stolen codes. Like magic, the large screen flipped to a live video stream from eight cameras. George and Marley recognised their school immediately.

"Hey, look George," Marley said pointing at the screen. "There's the work we did on that boring nature project." They spied the reception area, the playground, the school hall. Some were more distinct than others, but they clearly showed the whole school.

"I've never noticed the cameras before,"

Marley said, his eyes fixed on the screen.

"OK. I'm getting there now," Sam said. George glanced at his watch. Marley was quite happy sitting on the bed. It gave him an opportunity to daydream at Sam while she worked.

"Right," said Sam hitting the enter key with a flourish and spinning around in her chair to face the boys. "That's it. We have the connection. Let me show you. The image from the school cameras is quite good, and it looks like they have special lighting so even if it's pitch black you get a clear image of someone."

She pulled the cable from the phone and came to sit between them.

"OK. This is the app, it's on a hidden menu on the last page." Sam scrolled through the phone's front screen by swiping a few times.

"It's called 'Pickled' and if you tap on it, you'll be asked for a code. I put this on in case your Dad finds it, he still won't be able to get into it. The pin is one, one, one, one." Sam tapped the secret numbers, and the small screen split into six, each square showed a different view of the school.

"This is the live video from the school now," Sam explained getting excited about the technology. "The phone is recording continually and will keep the last seven days from each camera, then it writes over it again. Good isn't it?"

Marley nodded, glowing from head to foot.

"Marley, you need to look at the screen not at me," Sam said, smiling at him. Marley flushed and darted back at the screen. She continued, "So now you can catch Pickled Daniels out, it's ready to go."

"That's fantastic Sam," George said excitedly.

"Now we just need to get Pickled Daniels to do something in front of the camera, and we'll have the evidence to show Mrs T."

"That's right," said Sam. "Easy." Sam jumped up, grinning broadly.

George inspected the phone. Abruptly the video screens went black.

"What's happened?" George thrust the phone at Sam, his face furrowed.

"I don't know. Let me look." Sam replied, a look of concern spreading across her face. She plugged the phone back in.

"Goodness. It's a bug, or a virus or something. It isn't working how I thought it would. Listen, you'll have to give me more time." Sam was fidgeting with her mouse.

George glanced at Marley. Marley had his head in his hands.

"I knew this wouldn't work." Marley got up and paced the room. "This is terrible. This is really bad. What do we do now?"

"I don't know. It's late now. Look, we'd better get going before Jennie knows we're gone. And we need to get Dad's phone back," said George. "Can you work on it for the rest of the week Sam? Do you think you can fix it? It must be ready for the show on Saturday."

"OK George. I'll try and get it done by Friday night. But I can't promise anything."

"Friday night," said Marley with real concern, "That's the day before the show. We'll have no time to do anything." George pulled on Marley's top.

"OK, thanks Sam. Try your best."

"No problem," said Sam dejectedly. She had already spun back to her desk, drumming on the keyboard.

"Come on Marley let's go."

Marley got up sheepishly and turned to Sam. "Thanks, S...S...Sam."

"Bye Marley." He sighed.

It took George and Marley a record six minutes and thirty-four seconds to ride back.

Opening the back door gently, they heard the TV still on full volume from the living room. Peeling off their coats, Phoebe marched into the kitchen.

"Where've you been?" Phoebe demanded. "I'm going to tell Mum and Dad when they get back. You've been out for ages." She grumpily stormed off. George sprinted after her.

"Phoebe, wait." He grabbed her top. "Don't say anything to them." George's face was ashen.

"What do I get?" Phoebe replied, staring him in the eye. They stood face to face, Marley had never seen a little girl blackmailing someone before, it was fascinating.

"Erm...what do you want?" George said.

"I need some new butterfly hair clips, a necklace made of sweets and a pink ring," she said after serious consideration. She had her hands on her hips and her legs spread. She knew that's how you should stand in these situations from an TV show she'd seen. George looked at Marley, then back at Phoebe. Marley shrugged his shoulders.

"Look. I can give you five pounds from my money box, and you'll have to get the things you want. OK?"

"Deal." Phoebe smirked, holding out a hand for George to wearily shake.

21 A LOVELY TEA GUEST

It was the day before the big show and preparations were well underway. For Pickled Daniels that meant an early start. She stood in her garage lovingly appraising her beautiful collection of ghastly gadgets. She'd spent last night compiling a list of ideas to stop the show before it had started. She'd gathered everything together, checking each item one by one before moving them into the house. It was quite extensive:

One large melon (mouldy)

Two extremely rotten eggs

A miniature block of blue cheese (immensely smelly)

One box of ants (small - the box not the ants)

Amazonian Spiders (very black)

A pair of scissors (rusty)

One stink bomb (reserve)

Seven rats (grey? dyed black?)

Small cage (ferrets?)

Clock with timer

A ball of string

A tin of grease (small)
One marker pen (black)
A small tool kit
Three bottles of food dye (red, green, purple)
A mop and bucket

Pickled Daniels planned on attacking from all sides. It wasn't enough anymore to leave small traps, or slowly upset one of the Year Twos. With only one day before the show, she was going to put an end to the show once and for all. The pile of checked items was gradually growing when she heard a faint knock on her front door. She froze. No one ever visited her. Never. Ever. She had no family to speak of (apart from a distant cousin in Whitby who was probably dead).

Resting the filthy rat cage, she lumbered to the front door.

Proudly standing there with a broad smile on her face was Mrs T, holding Clive in her arms.

"Mrs Daniels, so sorry to bother you at home at this time of day. I just wanted to have a little word with you, it won't take long." Clive wriggled, eyeing up Pickled Daniels.

Pickled Daniels panicked. She mentally ran through what Mrs T would be eyeing up behind her. Did she have any of her ghastly 'props' on display? She didn't think so, but her palms moistened anyway.

"Can I come in?" Mrs T enquired, delivering Clive to the doormat.

"Erm...well. Mes just having me breakfast but I suppose so, could you wait a moment?" Pickled Daniels voice quivered. A bead of sweat appeared on her wrinkly brow.

She slammed the door, her head twitching with madness. Gathering the piles, she desperately threw them in cupboards anywhere she could find space. The rotten eggs whiffed in the kitchen, but she couldn't do anything about that now. She stuffed them frantically into the cutlery drawer. The rats were scurrying around in their cage. She gathered it up and placed the whole appalling appliance into the cupboard under the sink. She did a final sweep pushing the remaining lot from the table onto one of the seats and inserting it into under the table. Finally, everything was away.

"Please, please, what a pleasure for mes," Pickled Daniels said, almost bowing as she opened the door to Mrs T.

Mrs T hadn't been in the caretaker's house for a very long time, not since it had been sold off. In fact thinking back she hadn't actually been inside ever, previously she'd only got as far as the front porch. It looked like the place didn't get cleaned much, which was strange considering Mrs Daniels was the school cleaner.

"What is that Mrs Daniels?" Mrs T enquired, pointing at a giant, somewhat odd looking oil painting of an altogether loopy looking dog hanging in the hallway. It had a thick layer of dust over the gilt frame.

"Oh that.....," Pickled Daniels voice dipped a little, "it was me pet dog that was, years ago. Loved that dog I did. I give her a little kiss every now and then. I like to look at it, I can spend hours just staring at it sometimes. She don't talk back. She was called Fifi."

Mrs T appeared bewildered, hugging Clive even harder. "Erm...well how utterly spiffing, it's marvellous that you have such a....a.. wonderful outlook on life Mrs Daniels."

Pickled Daniels pulled out a chair to let Mrs T sit down.

"Thank you, Mrs Daniels. Listen, I'm sorry to bother you like this, but I think you'll be pleased with why I came," Mrs T said. Clive perched on her knee, sniffing. His damp nose up in the air.

Pickled Daniels wasn't used to social calls, she wondered what she was supposed to do. In the soap operas she occasionally watched, people drank tea when they visited others. But she didn't have tea, only water.

"Would you likes a water?" Pickled Daniels asked delicately, her eyes darting around the disgusting kitchen.

"That would be very kind Mrs Daniels, many thanks."

Pickled Daniels picked up a drying glass from the draining board and started to fill it.

"I think you'll be thrilled with what I'm about to tell you. You see, at this morning's assembly, we have an extraordinary guest coming in. And they are coming to see you, Mrs Daniels," Mrs T explained, smiling at Pickled Daniels back.

Pickled Daniels shot round with the glass in her hand, splashing Mrs T with water. Clive gave a yelp.

"Me!" she said, startled. "Whys they want to see me?"

"Stay calm Mrs Daniels. It's nothing to worry about." Mrs T dabbed the water now dribbling down her face. "It's Fire Fighter O'Gorman, he's coming to give you a bravery award for putting out the fire last week in the school, it will be extremely inspirational for the children, and we want to say a big thank you."

The blood drained from Pickled Daniel's head, and she swallowed the nauseous feeling in her throat. The last thing she wanted to do was spend more time at a school assembly with all the happy children. Her knees wobbled, and she steadied herself on the side of the sink. *I need a drink*, she thought to herself.

"I cants accepts its. It's not right. I don't likes the attention," Pickled Daniels pleaded.

"Nonsense," replied Mrs T firmly. "You showed inspiring courage and leadership that day, and it should be commended. The children love to have a role model, and they will all enjoy seeing you pick up your award. Of course, it's right."

Clive picked up the scent of the rats and strained from Mrs T's grip. His nose pointed towards the pans, and if his ears didn't deceive him, he thought he heard the slight scuttling noise of a rodent, he directed them towards the sink.

"Well I don't knows, I'll have to think about it," replied Pickled Daniels. Mrs T seemed determined, *how would she get out of this?*

Clive could contain himself no longer. In one movement he leapt from Mrs T's lap into the sink. He barked roughly into the plug hole while scrabbling with his front paws, desperately trying to dig a hole in the top. The shock of the movement made Pickled Daniels screech.

Mrs T shot out of her chair and rushed to the sink to prise him out.

"Clive!" Mrs T shrieked as she reached for him. "What on earth are you up to Clive. I do apologise, Mrs Daniels. He isn't normally this disobedient." She desperately grabbed Clive but he now had the scent of seven fully grown male rats in his nostrils, and he wanted them - with all his heart.

Pickled Daniels stood motionless. Over the barking of the dog, she could hear the scurrying of the rats under the sink. She needed to get Mrs T out of the kitchen, and more importantly out of the house, immediately. Mrs T had a firm grip on Clive now, but he had one paw glued to the plug hole.

There was only one thing for it. She grasped Mrs T around the middle and strained with all her strength to help with the removal of the little dog. They looked like a pensioners tug of war team. Clive was at full stretch but still clinging on. He knew a rat when he smelled one. Pickled Daniels gave another colossal heave.

Finally, Clive could grip no longer. The three of them shot back tumbling into a pile on the kitchen floor. Mrs T's legs were splayed everywhere, entangled with Pickled Daniels and finally, Clive curled up next to her. She pushed up on her arms sniffing the air, had the drains not been cleaned?

Pickled Daniels gave in, she just needed to get Mrs T out of the house. "I'd love to picks up mes award, that would be lovely," she said through gritted teeth.

Clive stepped off Mrs T's face.

"Erm....that's wonderful Mrs Daniels, we'll see you at eight forty-five then. Oh, and could you get in a bit early. Just a little work to do on the stage before the children arrive." Mrs T tried to get her composure back as she got to her feet, lightly brushing her front. She held Clive firmly in her arms, making a hasty exit.

Pickled Daniels heard the front door shut, everything was quiet again. She sank onto a seat and put her head in her hands. The only calming influence was the sound of rats gnawing under the sink.

22 IT'S TIME TO PLANT THE DUMMY, DUMMY

George and Marley planned to arrive especially early at school. Friday was their last chance to plant something to catch Pickled Daniels red-handed. George had persuaded Ernie to make a complete replica of his magic box without the intricate workings inside, he knew that it would be too tricky for Pickled Daniels to resist its beautiful carvings. Ernie hadn't really understood him at all when he had discussed the subject a few days ago.

"I need another box Ernie, not a fully working one, just one that looks like it's fully working," George had said to him early one evening.

"Fully parking? What does that mean? It's not got wheels lad."

"No Ernie. I said 'not working'. It doesn't need any of the insides. I just need a box with some simple carvings on the outside. So it looks like the real thing. Nothing too fancy. It shouldn't take too long." George was exasperated. It had taken him another half an hour to finally get through to Ernie precisely what he meant. Eventually, the penny dropped, and Ernie had grudgingly agreed to make a duplicate while complaining about the youth of today.

George and Marley were walking past the shops now, only a few streets away from school.

"It certainly looks important," Marley said while admiring the box, he ran his fingers over the delicate sculpture.

"Yer. It does doesn't it." George beamed. "It should do the job. She won't be able to resist it. We just need to make sure we see her so we can explain it."

"I don't ever want to speak to her." Marley looked concerned. "Do we have to?"

"Nor do I, but yes we have to. She needs to know that it's critical for my magic show. Have you got your script?"

Marley had finally decided that he was going to have a go at stand up comedy while juggling. He had no real talent for it, but his dad had encouraged him, thinking it would be good to have some comedy in the evening.

"Yep. Script and juggling balls in my bag ready for action." Marley grinned.

They walked the final few streets to school in

silence. Each knowing that the other was dreading the ensuing encounter with Pickled Daniels. As they approached the school gates George tried to dispense some advice, a frown forming on his brow.

"Look, act natural OK. She doesn't know that we know anything about her. Be casual. Relax."

Immediately Marley found it impossible to walk properly. Just knowing he had to act natural had made him act decidedly unnatural. Like when you're picked at in school assembly, and you have to walk to the front. He felt a pain in his chest; he was terrified of her. The school was deserted, with only a couple of children on the far playground kicking a ball around. They headed in. Marley was sure that his heartbeat could be heard outside his body. They tiptoed along in silence.

Inside the school, it was weirdly quiet. As they walked into the main school corridor George nudged Marley, he felt like he was in a spy film.

"Don't look directly up at it but keep walking." George was talking through gritted teeth like he was interacting with a ventriloquist's dummy. He grabbed Marley's arm. "There's a camera in the corner of this corridor. It's in a little box, and unless you know it's there, you won't notice it."

Marley had an urge to gaze up but kept his eyes focused. The hall was decked out to look like a real theatre rather than a drab school hall. The sides had big yellow sheets pinned near the roof, gathered into groups, so it gave the impression of an old Victorian music hall. Hefty curtains had been hung to match the rest of the room. The stage scenery had elaborately painted trees, it would be as though they were performing in a forest.

Mrs T was bending down through a gap in the stage.

"Further down Mrs Daniels. Not there. You need to connect the cable at the other end. Now, come on woman, get a grip." She was shrilling through the hole as if giving orders at a drive-thru takeaway.

Marley stared at George. "Pickled Daniels must be under there," he whispered. George nodded, his face reddening.

Mrs T straightened up tutting to herself, readjusting her blouse.

"Ah. George and Marley. All ready for the big show tomorrow, it's tremendously exciting," she clapped enthusiastically. They heard a bump, Pickled Daniels gave a yelp. Mrs T ignored it and went on.

"It will be a beautiful evening full of joy, inspiration, and entertainment. Mrs Walker has done a wonderful job in dressing the assembly room. Now boys, what have you got there? This looks very interesting."

Mrs T bounded over to them like an eager waiter, her eyes fixed on the magic box. Pickled Daniels crawled out from under the stage, coughing and spluttering - her bones creaking in the silence.

"It's not so nice under there. Full of spiders. The children wouldn't like it," she muttered to no one in particular, smiling at the thought of spiders and creepy crawlies landing on top of the children's heads during assembly. Spotting George and Marley, she fell silent, the grin slipping from her face.

"Come over and see this Mrs Daniels, it's wonderful."

Mrs T bent down to inspect the box. Grudgingly Pickled Daniels meandered over, eyes fixed on Marley. Marley gulped. Not knowing where to look he merely gazed up in the air. The wafting stink of damp clothing mixed with rotting fish permeated around the hall. The whiff was so revolting Marley turned to cover his nose.

"What's that?" Pickled Daniels prodded the magic box.

"Yes, what is it George?" enquired Mrs T.

"It's the main part of my show," George replied, exaggerating as much as possible to hook Pickled Daniels. "My Great Uncle made it. Inside are the magic workings to make things disappear in front of your eyes. I couldn't do anything without it."

"Well, your uncle certainly has a good deal of skill George, he's done a wonderful job."

"It's *really* important for me. Without this, I wouldn't be able to complete my act. I'd be devastated if anything happened to it." George exaggerated his best sad face.

Pickled Daniels was breathing heavily, staring at it.

"Look after it won't you," Pickled Daniels said, looking directly at George. He didn't know how to reply, so there was just an awkward silence while everyone just stared at the box. Everyone except Marley who was still focusing on the ceiling.

Finally, Mrs T broke the silence. "Yes, well. Let's get it safely into the back of the hall for safekeeping. Marley, what's in your bag?"

Marley didn't really want to talk. He played

with some invisible dirt with his foot.

"Erm. I'm...well...I've got my script and my juggling balls. I'm doing stand up comedy and juggling."

"That's equally wonderful," Mrs T gushed, over-enthusiastically, not having a clue what sort of act it was. "Right, well take them through and leave them with the rest of the props."

"I'll helps em," Pickled Daniels said. Marley glanced at George, gulping.

George carefully carried his magic box. Pickled Daniels didn't take her beady eyes off it as she followed George and Marley. Marley jogged on to catch up with George.

"She's just behind us."

"I know, I can smell her," George whispered. The back hall was designated as a changing room for the performers. Stacks of props and costumes lined the tables. Mounted on the ceiling was a small box, George knew this was the camera, he nudged Marley.

"There," he whispered, using his eyes to signal the position of the box.

"What?" Marley asked, confused.

Pickled Daniels caught up with them before George had a chance to say anything. She sneezed, sending a torrent of spit onto the back of Marley's head.

"Oh, so sorry, seems to always happen don't it" Pickled Daniels said, smiling broadly. She spun round to check Mrs T hadn't followed them, her manner changed as soon as she was sure they were alone.

"Right yous two," she said pointing a gnarled finger at them. "What's you up to? I seen you talking in the playground together about me and you've been sniffing around the staffroom. I hate kids watching me. Mes don't like it. Something fishy is going on and I'm going to find out what it is. WHAT YOU UP TO?"

She pushed her face even further into Marley's personal space. So close, in fact, he could see all horrid warts all over her face, and the slight outline of a moustache.

Pickled Daniels waited, her dank rum breath drifting up Marley's nostrils. Neither George nor Marley knew how to get out of this. Marley's legs were shaking like a jackhammer.

Mrs T suddenly appeared at the door – George let out a breath, Pickled Daniels stepped back, "Yes I would be happy to help you both set-up in the evening, I loves to help the children when I can."

Mrs T strode over. "How wonderful Mrs

Daniels, that is very kind. Isn't that kind of Mrs Daniels?"

They didn't know what to say.

"Erm...but...ermmm," Marley stammered trying to get out that Pickled Daniels wasn't kind at all, but an evil, old stout who needed to be stopped. Marley gulped.

"Erm..yes, that is very kind of Mrs Daniels," repeated George.

"Good, wonderful." Mrs T turned to Pickled Daniels. "Thank you for your help this morning Mrs Daniels. You'll need to go and open up the rest of the school, it's nearly registration time. I'll take care of George and Marley."

Pickled Daniels ambled out, the hideous smell wafting after her.

"OK boys, where shall we put your props?" chimed Mrs T eagerly. George knew this was their chance, they needed to make sure their props were directly in the line of the camera, he had to get the altercation with Pickled Daniels out of his mind and focus on the task at hand.

George had calculated that the third table from the back would offer the best chance of catching something on film. He started to walk towards it carrying his fake magic box.

"I think this would be best." George plonked

the box on the table, adjusting the position so that it was in-line with the camera.

"No George, I believe that Evie has reserved that as she has a large big bird costume she needs to store, her name should be on a label there? Can you see it?"

George spied a white sticker on the top of the table with the words "RESERVED - EVIE" written on it. This was their one chance to catch Pickled Daniels, he had to have this position, no others would have such a good view of the camera. He placed a hand over the sticker, slowly picking it off while distracting Mrs T by pulling the box around the table to make some noise.

"I don't think so, I can't see anything." George shouted a little, his ears turning red as he worked at the label with his finger."I think she has that table in the corner." George pointed at a spare table with nothing on it, his whole face now glowing.

"Oh....erm.... yes, well that must be it if there's no name on this one," agreed Mrs T. George finally had the label up, screwing it into a little ball.

Marley pulled out his juggling balls and script, laying them out neatly next to the magic box. George completed one final box adjustment. He stepped back and admired the room, he had no doubt that his magic box was the star. It would be just too much for Pickled Daniels not to be drawn to it.

The trap was set.

23 A NICE AWARD FOR THE GORGEOUS MRS DANIELS

Another tedious assembly started at eight forty-five, the children sat on the chairs already set out for the talent show. It was a rare treat, they usually had to sit cross-legged on the floor while only the teachers got the pleasure of seats around the edge of the hall. Children talked excitedly until Mrs T placed her finger on her lips which was the signal to be quiet.

"Now children, I know everyone is overwhelmed with the outstanding show we have planned for tomorrow, I'll be discussing this later in assembly. But first I have some points to announce which you should all be very proud about." Mrs T paused for dramatic effect. "As you know we had a major incident in the school nine days ago which could have turned out very nasty indeed. I am, of course, referring to the small fire. But we had a good outcome and to discuss this in more detail I would like to introduce to you, Firefighter O'Gorman."

Firefighter O'Gorman's massive frame

stepped out from behind the curtain, he was a formidable figure, in his smart uniform and badges - he clenched a small plaque. Everyone clapped, he was enormous standing next to Mrs T.

"Fire is not a joke," Firefighter O'Gorman stated in a sombre tone. George and Marley started to giggle. O'Gorman's voice was the deepest and most boring voice they'd ever heard.

"I repeat, fire is not a joke." This took the situation to a new level, George and Marley glanced at each other, biting their lips to suppress the giggles. When someone says that something is not a joke (especially in a school assembly) it immediately becomes funny.

"We take a lot of care to protect municipal buildings such as this one, your safety is of paramount importance to us in the fire service. Margaret has kindly..." The mention of Mrs T's first name was the final straw, both of them burst out laughing. He had broken the cardinal rule of school etiquette, using a teacher's first name in front of the children.

Mrs Tinsley wasn't happy, first glaring at O'Gorman and then casting her teacher radar to see who was laughing. She gave George and Marley *"one of her looks"*, which was enough to shut them up. Marley gulped. O'Gorman continued, "Margaret has kindly asked me to say a few words about fire safety..."

Backstage, Pickled Daniels was shaking. She peeped through a gap in the curtain and saw the rows and rows of happy children concentrating on the words of the serious fireman. She felt sick at their happiness. Pulling out her bottle, she took a few quick swigs to calm her nerves.

O'Gorman seemed to go on for hours, even the initial funniness had worn off. Now all of the children had a glazed expression on their faces as O'Gorman came to the end of his drab speech.

"...and so we also rely on members of the public to be vigilant to call us in the case of emergency. We do warn against people tackling fires themselves and ask them to leave it to the professionals. But sometimes we have to give praise to someone who has had no thought for themselves but has had tremendous thought for others. Someone who is brave enough to step up to the situation and says to themselves, there are children's lives at risk here and I have to do something. Yes, your school was lucky to have someone like that here on the day of your fire, your brave and heroic Mrs Daniels."

Firefighter O'Gorman turned, clapping furiously. Mrs T joined in, followed slowly by the rest of the teachers and eventually all the children were clapping loudly.

Pickled Daniels swallowed, venturing from behind the curtain, wiping the sweat from her damp brow. Mrs T doubled her clapping rate when she came into view. Pickled Daniels slowly tramped across the stage. O'Gorman winced a little from the smell, he coughed to give himself an excuse to raise his hand to his nose.

"Erm...Mrs Daniels," he gathered his composure and turned to face her directly. "This award is from the Fire Service. Last week you were brave and selfless, and you are commended for your actions. This small plaque is a thank you from us all." Handing it over he gave another huge clap.

Pickled Daniels mind was doing somersaults. The hall was silent, all eyes on her, waiting. She felt incredibly uncomfortable. Her eyes focused on the stage as she tried to think what to say. Her mouth was dry, she desperately needed another drink.

"Thank yous. I was just doing me job, you don't have to thank me," Pickled Daniels blurted out. She couldn't think of anything more - so merely turned to scuttle off the stage, waving a wrinkled hand.

Feeling sick from the overall cheeriness of the children Pickled Daniels knew she had to make herself feel better. If she didn't stop the show now, she never would. This was the ideal opportunity, everyone in assembly in one place. Gathering up her beaten carrier bag she made for the changing rooms.

Laid out in designated piles were all the costumes, props, scripts and equipment for the talent show. She smiled sweetly to herself, this was perfect, she could still hear Mrs T droning on in assembly.

"Oh, wouldn't it be terrible if something were to happen to all these things," she said sarcastically, rubbing her hands in delight. Trawling the room, she prodded and poked.

There were clown costumes, dance outfits, a large tea chest, musical instruments, pirate clothes, a pantomime horse's head and big bundles of balloons. She slunk about, assessing what to do. Gingerly, she picked up a clarinet, worried that the children's happiness germs might affect her. In the top of the instrument, she picked at the reed, eventually popping it out and pocketing it. That's a good start, she thought, can't play it now.

Now she gained confidence. Reaching the year two ballet costumes she picked one up and plucked gently at a rogue thread on the side, drawing harder she made a large hole in the bottom of the outfit. She smiled widely. Prowling around she fiddled with other props, making sure not to do too much, she wanted it to appear like everything was in order but to have these small things go wrong for the children.

Spying George's magic box proudly displayed, a broad smile broke onto her face - she crouched down to have a good look. Her thin nose lightly touching it.

"This looks a bit delicate," she said smirking. Extending a single damp finger, she nudged the side of the box, slowly it moved across the table. It made a subtle grinding sound as it edged across the surface. Pickled Daniels gave a quick look around to make sure that no one was looking and, with a final small heave, the box teetered, see-sawed a little, then finally fell - crashing to the ground. It ruptured in two, sending splinters cascading over the floor.

"Oh dear, what a shame," Pickled Daniels whispered to herself, grinning like a gnome. Spotting Marley's juggling balls she pocketed one, leaving only four. Leafing through his script, she tore out some pages.

Mrs T was winding up her speech. Chairs were scraped as the pupils got up to leave and chatter began. Suddenly Pickled Daniels was glued to the spot, her only way out was back through the stage door to the other half of the hall! In approximately twenty seconds some of the children and staff could potentially be arriving, and here she was surrounded by broken props and battered costumes!

Pickled Daniels closed her eyes, trying some deep meditation to stop the shakes. Someone was running across the stage about to come through the door. She had to hide. Palms sweating, she peered under the table, not enough room for hiding she thought. The door opened, she'd run out of time!

Pickled Daniels stared at Phoebe. She sighed with relief, it wasn't Mrs T. She could talk her way out of this. Phoebe stepped in oblivious to what Pickled Daniels had been up to.

"Hello Mrs Daniels," Phoebe said brightly.

"Where shall I put this?" Phoebe held up her costume.

Pickled Daniels smiled.

"I'll hang that for you, give it here," Pickled

Daniels said snatching it out of her hand.

"Thank you, Mrs Daniels," Phoebe replied skipping out of the room.

I'll certainly take this, thought Pickled Daniels to herself, stuffing the costume down the front of her shawl. Clutching her plaque, she did a complete turn around the room to survey the devastation she'd left.

That should make a lot of them extremely miserable, she thought, happily closing the door.

24 I DON'T FEEL LIKE DANCING

"Don't eat so fast George, you'll give yourself indigestion," said mum.

He tried to slow down but Marley and Sam were due at six and he didn't want to be late. Ernie was cutting up his food painfully slowly.

"Is my magic box ready Ernie?" George asked loudly.

"What?" Ernie shouted back.

"Is my box ready?" George hollered.

"What box?" Ernie screwed up his face.

"My magic box, the one you built for me. The show is tomorrow."

Dad walked into the kitchen. "Don't worry, Son, it's all working, Ernie and I tested it earlier. Do you have your ingredients more importantly? You can't perform baking magic, whatever that is, without them." He smiled.

George had his mouth jammed full of fish fingers so pointed to the side of the kitchen. Stacked up in a neat pile was the flour, eggs and sugar with some freshly baked cakes next to them.

"Oh. These look good," his Dad said, picking up a cake, mouth opening like a shark ready to take a bite.

"*Dad...stop*." George spluttered fish finger everywhere. "I need them for tomorrow as well, they're the ones which will be in the magic box."

"Oh yer, I forgot about that." Dad placed the cake back on the stack.

"**Looking forward to the show tomorrow Ernie?**" shouted Dad. "A big night out for you isn't it?"

"Crow? What you talking about?"

"Not crow, show. Why would I be asking you - are you looking forward to the crow tomorrow? **The show, you're coming to the show aren't you?** The one George and Phoebe are in?" explained Dad.

"Oh yes, I'd love to."

Dad rolled his eyes and got on with preparing his own tea.

"I've been practising my dance moves George," his dad said, gyrating his feet on the kitchen floor.

"No Dad, I told before, please don't embarrass me," George said, getting up to put his plate on the side.

"Embarrass you? Not likely. Impress you? Yes. I'll have you know I was break dancing champion at school," he added doing a kick in the air.

George was in no mood for discussion. The doorbell rang. George raced to let Marley in.

"Quick come in, we haven't long. It's just Marley, we're going up to my room."

"Where's Sam?" Marley asked, smiling like a buffoon as they raced upstairs.

"Not here yet, you would have noticed if she was."

"What do you mean?"

"Sit here and look out the front window, you'll soon see." They looked like a couple of hapless meerkats waiting for her arrival.

"I don't see anything," Marley said after a minute.

"Wait," George replied, focusing intently on the view down the road. After a minute Marley spotted a faint flashing light at the very end of the street. The glowing moved closer; Sam was sat astride a sizeable red mountain bike which had been adapted to Sam's exact specifications.

It was a magnificent sight.

Across every surface were strips of multi-coloured bulbs which were pulsing at different rates, providing a stunning light show as she rode. Sam had an ear-piece in, talking. On the front of the handlebars was a miniature computer monitor which Sam was touching to activate different light patterns.

But the best thing by far were the speakers, Sam had flat panel speakers attached all around which she had linked to a sound generator, so her bike had the exact sound of a motorbike. As she came roaring down the road anyone not looking up would have sworn she was a riding a Harley Davidson. Not only did it sound like a genuine motorbike, it looked like one, as Sam had added a small smoke machine which puffed out bellows of mist in time with the engine noise. This was too much for Marley, not only was she possibly the best looking and most intelligent girl he had ever met, now she was riding the best bike he'd ever seen.

"See, told you," George said, grinning at Marley. They waved as she pushed her bike up the front path and rang on the bell.

"Hi ya, George," Sam said, pulling off her cycling helmet letting her long hair fall down. Marley stood behind George staring trance-like at Sam.

"I've got some great news for you two," She took the rucksack off her back.

George's dad came into the hallway and saw Sam. They all fell silent.

"Hiya, Sam, what you doing here? Did someone die, why the silence?" he asked.

"Hi, I've come to see George." She replied sheepishly.

George's dad looked perplexed. "What you up to George?"

"Oh, it's nothing Dad, Sam was going to show us some computer programming for a project at school," he replied trying to reassure him nothing untoward was going on. "Come on Sam lets go upstairs." Sam noticed the smartphone on the hall table. They were going to need that. She pulled his sleeve.

"Didn't you say we could listen to some music in your room," she said somewhat stiltedly nodding towards the phone on the table.

"Oh yes", replied George suddenly realising what she meant, "Dad, could I borrow your phone for a little bit to listen to some music in my room."

"No, I don't think so. I'm waiting for an important call from work." George's heart missed a beat, they needed the phone.

"Come on Dad, we won't play with it and if there's a call we'll shout for you." George tried to sound genuine.

"I'll make sure they look after it," Sam added smiling serenely.

None of them moved a muscle, it felt like forever before George's dad reached a decision.

"Go on then. But be careful with it, and I need some battery left. Bring it down if it rings." He handed it to George. Sam gave Marley a relieved smile.

In George's room, Sam set up her laptop.

"OK, the good news..." Sam looked really pleased with herself.

"What is it?" George asked plonking himself down on the bed. Marley joined him.

"Well let me show you. First, you know you kindly acquired the log in codes from your headmistress..." said Sam breathlessly.

"Acquired? You mean stole!" Marley butted in.

"Well, I've managed to get into the system myself. It was easy in the end."

"Are you saying there was no need for us to break into Mrs T office and steal the codes?" asked Marley slowly.

"That's what I'm saying," replied Sam smiling broadly.

"Well thanks a lot, all of that for nothing." Marley huffed, crossing his arms. "We very nearly got caught doing that."

"And you did great Marley, it gave me a couple of extra days to work out how to record and document everything, so it wasn't wasted. And I've sorted out the bug in the system. It all works now." Sam beamed at Marley.

George handed her the phone and they

huddled around it as the app launched. The screen showed the live video streams of their school.

"OK. I need to show you something." Sam said. She turned to her laptop. "I just need to get the times from here which I noted down."

George and Marley waited, spellbound.

"Right. Look at this." She pulled a crumpled note out of her trousers and then entered yesterday's date.

"Cool. Now the time," Sam said entering nine sixteen into the interface, reading from the paper.

"Watch this." She propped the phone in front of them so they could all see. The screen showed the dressing room. It was empty.

"Nothing's happening," said Marley a little disappointed.

"Wait a moment," Sam said, not taking her eyes off the screen. Pickled Daniels appeared at the side of the screen carrying a bag.

"Keep watching."

Pickled Daniels was rubbing her hands like an itchy insect, talking to herself all the while, poking the props as she walked around the room. Then her destructive spree began.

"Yes, see...We were right!" hollered Marley

grabbing George. "She's messing up all those costumes."

"Wait, it gets better," Sam added, grinning wildly.

Pickled Daniels had reached the magic box, she crouched down with her wet nose right up to it.

"What's she doing?" asked George. He soon got his answer, they watched as she slowly pushed it across the table until it shattered on the floor. George jumped up from the bed in a state of real excitement.

"We've done it. This is the evidence we need," he said. "This is great. We've done it Marley. All those times when the unexplained happened, this proves it all." George leaned over and hugged Sam.

"Thanks Sam, we couldn't have done it without you." Marley said awkwardly leaning in for a hug as well.

"It's not done yet," Sam replied, bringing them back down to earth. "We have the evidence but now you need to show your headmistress."

"I've thought about that," said George, "I'm going to show Mrs T all the evidence tomorrow evening before the show. Dad will be there so I can use his phone and both Mrs T and Pickled

Daniels will be around, it will be the perfect opportunity."

"Good idea," Sam replied picking up the phone and closing the utility. She handed the phone to George.

"Just make sure your dad doesn't lose his phone before tomorrow evening, you know what he's like!"

25 THE SMELL OF THE GREASEPAINT

The evening of the show had finally arrived, and the Ferris family was in full *"getting ready"* mode. George's Dad was flying all over searching for his trousers and shirt, yelling at anyone who would listen. Phoebe was busy practising her ballet moves waiting for everyone to be ready. Mum was helping Uncle Ernie find his coat and hat. George was merely nervous, pacing the living room.

After Sam had left last night, George had gone through his act over and over again. Mixing cake ingredients and then magically 'baking' his cakes in the magic box all within his allocated four-minute slot, which wasn't going to be easy - but it certainly was going to be messy. He was convinced though that he would be a triumph. They were soon bundled into the car and heading off to the school; George's Dad finally fully clothed.

Pickled Daniels was in a foul mood. She had been at school early in the morning under strict instructions from Mrs T to clean, tidy and generally prepare for the show before anyone even arrived for breakfast club.

She had complained bitterly about this but then turned it to her advantage. She needed time to prepare her final wicked plans for the evening, so she'd taken advantage of being there while the school was empty and she'd managed to place everything where she needed it.

The food dye was in the large tea and coffee boilers ready for the half-time break. She'd released the swarm of giant south Amazonian spiders at the back of the hall which she figured would scamper to the back rows in time for the start of the show, plus ghastly giant rats (with a timer for their cage to open during the interval). In the dining room, large blocks of rotten blue cheese, mixed with two rotten eggs - the stink was already permeating, and finally, a large, over-ripe, melon forced down the toilets causing a blockage.

It was an hour before the start of the show, most of the children would be turning up any minute. Pickled Daniels tramped around the hall prodding and kicking chairs out of position. Her stomach twisted and squirmed in knots - she was actually starting to feel mildly excited. Any time now the children would see the conked out props and broken costumes and burst into tears, and she'd get to watch it all!

There would be no option but for Mrs T to cancel the show. She would be back at home with a nice glass of sherry in hand by eight o'clock.

She stood at the side of the stage just close enough to hear the disappointment from the back room when it all got underway. *What bliss to see them all wailing.*

Mrs T and Mrs Walker strode through the hall adjusting seats as they went. Clive was at Mrs T's feet with his tail wagging.

"There you are Mrs Daniels, how you feeling?" Mrs T marched towards her with a concerned look on her face.

Pickled Daniels blinked out of her daydream.

"I am getting one of my little headaches, I can feel it coming on." She didn't want to sound too bad as she really wanted to stay to hear the six-year-olds crying.

"Well, never mind that. I have a list as long as my arm here for you to do. Myself and Mrs Walker need to check the audiovisual equipment. Can you check the kitchens, please? We need to make sure all the cups are out, and the parents who have volunteered for manning the tea stall understand the rota. Everything must be in tip-top condition tonight Mrs Daniels, this is a showcase event for the school. Nothing must go wrong." Mrs T sniffed, wiggling her nose.

"Well, I was just doing something here," Pickled Daniels indicating her broom.

"Never mind that now," Mrs T replied. "That can be done just before the show starts. Run along now."

"I suppose so." Pickled Daniels grudgingly wandered off kicking some dirt on the floor as she went. Clive gave a little growl, the rat incident still playing on his mind.

The Ferris family arrived at the school gates five minutes later. The car park was filling up fast. The central problem was Uncle Ernie, it took him an eternity to get in and out of the car. George was getting impatient, he needed to talk to Mrs T.

"Dad, could I borrow your phone for a few minutes? I want to play music with Marley while we're getting ready," George asked as Dad levered Uncle Ernie from the front seat.

"Not now, Son. Come on Ernie, push yourself up," he said, bending into the car and putting Ernie's arms around his neck to give him some support.

George needed the phone! "Just for ten minutes Dad," he pleaded.

"Leave your father be, George," His mum butted in, coming round from the other side of the car. "You can see he's busy. You won't need music, there'll be so much going on anyway. You'd better get your magic box." She opened the boot and pulled out the genuine magic box. Dad stood up unable to manhandle Ernie from the car, he patted his pocket.

"I haven't got my phone anyway son. Must have left it at home". He bent down again to have another attempt at extracting Ernie. George's world stopped.

"What! You haven't got your phone? Why haven't you got your phone? You must have your phone. Where is it?" demanded George, his voice rising to manic levels.

"George. Don't be so rude to your father. You know how forgetful he can be. He won't need it tonight anyway." said George's mum now going in to grab another of Ernie's thrashing arms.

George spotted Marley with his parents on the other side of the car park.

"Erm...sorry Dad, for shouting...OK...I've got to think...I mean...I've got to go, I'll see you later," he said shooting off.

"OK. Good luck," shouted his mother to his departing feet. George joined Marley.

"I haven't got the phone, my dad's forgotten it," he whispered to Marley walking across the car park. Marley turned ashen.

"What do you mean you haven't got the phone? Without that we haven't got the evidence. Why didn't you make sure your dad brought it with him. This is a disaster." George never usually saw Marley get angry.

"I can't, can I? I took his phone without his permission, he would kill me if he found out."

"What are you two gossiping about?" Marley's mum asked.

"Nothing Mrs Matthews, just rehearsing."

Mrs T and Pickled Daniels were welcoming people in, Mrs T had Clive under one arm, squashing him like a set of bagpipes. She waved her spare arm, signalling for them to come over.

"Ah George there you are. I meant to catch you before you came in...I...erm..." it seemed like Mrs T was, for once, lost for words. She glared at his magic box. "Your box ....broke...Erm…this makes no sense. You see to have a box with you there. It's just I'm sorry to say that there has been a little bit of an incident. You see we went into the changing room before everyone started to arrive and your magic box has unfortunately been in a minor accident, I'm afraid it must have been perched on the edge of the table, and it's fallen off, you see the whole thing just smashed on the floor."

She paused waiting for a reaction; she had assumed he would burst into tears. Pickled Daniels smirked waiting for the waterworks to start. Clive's eyes were firmly on Marley. Clive never forgot a face. After a pause, George spoke.

"It's no problem. I've got this one." George smiled brightly presenting his second magic box in front of him. Pickled Daniels scowled at the box, utterly puzzled about the situation. *Had he fixed the broken one that quickly? Why did he have another one? It can't be possible? Why did the little twerp look so happy?* Her mind went into overdrive. She needed a drink. Gulping back nausea.

"Oh, well...erm...that is good news. I was worried about it, but you seem to have everything in hand," replied Mrs T with a wide smile.

If Pickled Daniels had not been standing right in front of him, it would have been the perfect time to spill the beans, but George didn't feel confident. Marley looked around the playground, trying to distract himself.

Across the other side of the car park came the roar of a large motorbike, every head turned.

"Who on earth is that? What an extraordinary racket." Mrs T searched for the culprit. Clive barked, he didn't know what at, he just thought he should.

"That'll be my cousin, Sam," George said as her push bike rumbled into view. She came to a halt in front of them with a final puff of smoke.

"Well, make sure he parks it with the rest of the motorbikes," said Mrs T disappearing with Pickled Daniels in tow.

Sam pulled off her bike helmet.

"Sam. Thank goodness, you're here. We've got a problem. Dad's forgotten his phone. We haven't any evidence. Everything's going wrong. You'll need to go back to our house and get his phone."

"What, now? I haven't got time. The performance will be starting soon. I'll never get there and back before the start of the show." Sam scanned her smart watch.

"Please Sam. You're our only hope," pleaded Marley, doe-eyed.

George held out his door key to her like a carrot for a donkey.

Finally, the show got underway. Mum, Dad and Ernie were sat in a line on the second row smiling up at the stage. The curtains opened to a drum roll revealing Mrs Walker dressed as a giant squirrel. The audience burst into spontaneous applause as she introduced the show.

"What's that smell?" whispered George's dad nudging his wife as soon as Mrs Walker had started. He sniffed the air.

"I thought it was you," Mrs Ferris replied, not taking her eyes off the stage.

"That's funny, I thought it was you," he whispered back smiling.

Pretty soon the whole audience noticed the ghastly stink. Pickled Daniels combination of blue cheese and rotten eggs, combined with the last minute addition of damp towels and ferret droppings was finally having the desired effect. Mrs Walker went on to explain that they had a few problems with the costumes but that the show must go on as the children had been so looking forward to the evening.

At the curtains Pickled Daniels was fuming, nothing seemed to be working. In the school entrance, she had released an additional two hundred, extra-black Australian spiders which she had been hand rearing since last October - but it had done nothing, they'd simply scrambled out of the door for freedom. One child even picked one up to show her parents. *When did children start liking spiders?* Pickled Daniels sulked. The smell was beginning to work though, but it needed extra pressure to get the scents moving around a bit. She'd fetched a set of ancient bellows from her bungalow, to permeate the stench, but still everyone was in her precious school.

But worst of all were the props she'd destroyed. The teachers had all rallied round and fixed or borrowed things to help the children, some of them had even been happier with their 'new' costumes than the one she'd destroyed.

Backstage George was sitting with Marley dressed in costume. Well, Marley wasn't really in costume, he was wearing the clothes he'd turned up in, but he found he was less nervous if he thought of it as a costume. George was dressed in a purple velvet apron and cape, which he thought gave the impression of someone who wanted to bake, but was also a member of the magic circle.

Mrs T swept into the room with Clive jogging behind her, she had a clipboard and was ticking off names as she went. *This is our opportunity* thought George.

"Mrs Tinsley?" George said, rather quietly,

peering around to check no one else was listening.

"Yes George," she said, not taking her eyes off the clipboard as she continued to make notes.

"Erm...it's just that..." George didn't know how to start. Marley was no help, he just shuffled, embarrassed, behind him.

"Yes, what is it, George? I'm busy." Mrs T looked up. "I haven't much time as I need to check the kitchens..." She waited. It was all somewhat intimidating.

"Well...you know that my magic box was smashed." George replied slowly, his face slowly turning red.

"Yes. I know." Mrs T was losing patience.

"Well...it wasn't an accident, you see Mrs Daniels deliberately broke it. She pushed it onto the floor. And she stole one of Marley's juggling balls, ripped out a page in his script. And she tore costumes. She did everything." George crossed his hands for effect, his forehead now crimson.

The words had tumbled out of him, and he felt much better for it. Mrs T was silent. She looked at George and then at Marley. Butterflies fluttered in George's tummy, they'd finally done it. They had sorted out that horrid old lady for all the nasty things she had done to children.

Eventually Mrs T spoke. She said only two words, very sternly.

"What rot."

She paused gathering her thoughts, face contorted in anger. "I will not have you say those things about Mrs Daniels, George. After all she has done for this school over many years, I have nothing but high praise for her. And to think she saved you all from what could have become a dreadful incident with the fire. Without her, this show would not be taking place."

"But..." George tried to interject.

"No more, George! I don't want to hear another word on the subject." She marched out. Clive gave them a nod and a small growl, jogging after Mrs T.

"Well that's it then," sighed Marley. "Why didn't you say we had the evidence?"

"Because we haven't, have we," George said dejectedly.

26 THE WORLD'S FIRST BAKING MAGICIAN

George's Dad was enjoying the evening. Phoebe's ballet dance had gone down a storm in the first half, and even the purple tea at the break hadn't bothered him, it had caused a lot of commotion amongst the other parents, but he had enjoyed the whole episode.

The boy's toilets had been blocked, so they had all been forced to share the one tiny toilet near the school entrance but that was normal, there were always things going wrong in the school thought Dad. They settled back, ready for the second half, George was on first. George's Dad inhaled deeply, the smell was definitely getting worse.

The hall went dark, a dry ice machine started. Dad smiled knowing that this was George's big entrance. George's mum munched on some popcorn cramped next to Ernie. Slowly the curtain peeled back with much huffing and puffing from Pickled Daniels who had been tasked with pulling the curtain rope. George stepped onto the stage with his hands apart waiting for applause, he didn't get much - just a laugh from the back of the audience. It's quite funny seeing an eleven-year-old boy in a purple apron and cape if you're an eight-year-old girl.

On stage, a small table was set with his baking ingredients to one side and the magic box on the other. George stepped forward talking to the audience. A projector cast an image onto the back of the stage, a mystical swirling pattern which George felt added to the effect of his magic.

"I am the world's first baking magician," announced George proudly, picking up a large bowl and depositing some flour. George had timed it, so some soft music started up. Suddenly one of the curtains fell back in front of the stage obscuring Georges act. A collective gasp went up. Mrs T scrambled up from her seat.

"Sorry everyone," she shouted going backstage.

Pickled Daniels was pulling the drawstring backwards and forwards beaming to herself.

"What on earth is going on Mrs Daniels," Mrs T barked.

"So sorry Mrs Tinsley, the cord broke you see." Pickled Daniels showed half a drawcord hanging in the air. She had managed to kick her scissors away just in time. "I can't reach it now. Not with my back and everything. He'll have to stop and go home." Her face twisted in innocence.

"Don't be so silly Mrs Daniels. I'll sort this out. Well quick. Help me with the step ladder." Mrs T precariously climbed the steps.

On stage, George had adapted. He had brought his bowl to the right-hand side of the table. George revealed the baking ingredients using large hand gestures like a proper magician. By the time Mrs T had sorted the curtain he had finished with the mixing and had begun depositing dollops of cake mix into holders. Flour covered the stage and himself, but it seemed to have kept the audience entertained. As the half curtain raised again, the audience applauded.

George was approaching the end of his act. Music pulsed louder and faster, the projected pattern swirled, George put six uncooked cakes onto a plate, perching them on the magic box. In time with a loud bang from the music George lifted his arms and shouted 'bake off' as loud as he could, waving a black wand. The swirling projection flared white, then black - a spotlight switched on. George flipped the switch on the back of the box, all at once the audience could see six perfectly formed and risen cakes. The audience erupted into spontaneous applause. He'd done it.

Backstage Marley was fidgeting. He'd practised his lines while trying out some juggling.

Hearing the applause for George, he realised he had no chance of doing that well, his stomach performed nervous somersaults. George rushed into the room clutching his box, covered head to toe in flour.

"Well done. I heard the clapping. Listen, we need to talk about Pickled Daniels." Marley glanced around nervously.

"Why, what's happened?"

"What's happened?" Marley was exasperated.

"Don't you think it's odd what's happening tonight? There's a terrible smell in the hall, the tea was purple at break, there are spiders in the front hall, the toilets are blocked, the curtains won't work. She's trying to ruin the whole evening."

"Yer, I've noticed the smell," replied George holding his nose.

"This is no coincidence, George." Marley had real concern in his voice. "I saw her walking backstage looking at some of the other costumes, I'm sure she was looking to steal them. And now it's all too late, Mrs T didn't believe us, and now that horrible Pickled Daniels is going to get away with it. And what happened to Sam? She was meant to get the phone."

"No idea. I haven't heard from her. I think we've blown our chance of ever exposing Pickled

Daniels." George said gloomily, like a man destined to eat school dinners for the rest of his life.

Mrs Walker peered around the backstage door.

"You're on now Marley," she said. Marley gathered his juggling balls, dropping one in the process.

The evening was drawing to a close, and the final street dance act was on. Children gathered ready to line the stage for Mrs T's closing address. George and Marley looked out of the wings desperately searching for Sam. Phoebe, still in her tutu, pushed her way in front. Pickled Daniels stood on the opposite side of the stage looking miserable. As the act finished, Mrs T came forward clapping enthusiastically.

"Well done to our street dance group, excellent performance. Now, the final part of the show. You've all seen how well the children have performed this evening and now it's your turn. I'm sure we have hidden talent out there in the audience. As part of our finale would any of the parents like to show us their talents?"

The room was silent apart from some mumbling in the back.

"Come on, don't be shy now. I'm sure you have something to show us. Anyone?" Mrs T reviewed the throng.

The room remained stubbornly silent. More murmurs from the back. A hand shot up from the second row.

"Ah yes, we have a volunteer. Excellent, Mr Ferris please come up."

George groaned. Phoebe turned bright crimson and looked at George as if to say, 'do something'. *We will never, ever live this down* thought George, *I'm going to have to change schools and probably my name as well.* He'd never been so embarrassed in his entire life. This had to be a joke, but it wasn't. George's dad bustled along the row and made his way onto the stage grinning broadly. He stood proudly next to Mrs T. George closed his eyes to try and make the whole embarrassing thing disappear.

"Thank you for volunteering, Mr Ferris. Now, what will you be performing tonight?" Phoebe stood with her mouth open, mortified.

"Well Mrs Tinsley, as a teenager I was quite a mover, my breakdancing was legendary," George's Dad replied looking at the audience like a bewildered baboon. There were a few laughs as he certainly didn't look like a legendary breakdancer now, or any sort of dancer for that matter. Mrs T wasn't even sure what break dancing was but went along with it. She'd expected someone to give a reading from Dickens or recite a poem, she certainly hadn't expected one of the parents to want to dance.

"Oh, dancing Mr Ferris. How frightfully fabulous!" She tried to put a brave face on it.

"OK, well erm...I'm sure we can do something. We have no music though."

George's dad fished in his pockets.

"Hang on, I have the music on my phone, you can plug it into the projector." He pushed both his hands in even further and patted his rear pockets. "Of goodness, I'm sorry, I haven't got my phone." The hall was silent, Dad looked crestfallen.

Then the most extraordinary thing happened. The hall doors burst open. A deafening bike roared as Sam came crashing down the central aisle. Smoke poured out as she came to a halt at the projector, the audience gasped as the bike's motor cut out with a little growl. Sam stepped off like a cowboy at a western, whipping off her helmet.

"Sorry to interrupt," she said surveying everyone, sweat dripping, "but your phone's here uncle, it must have fallen out of your pocket."

Marley gave a sideways glance at George, giving him a thumbs up. Sam barged her way to the projector.

"I'll sort it out for you, you just get ready to dance."

Mrs T was slightly perturbed by all the unorthodox behaviour but let it carry on. "Dim the lights please," Mrs T barked to the back of the hall.

The stage was pitch black. George's dad struck a pose, ready to launch into his killer dance moves. George stood immobile at the edge of the stage, hoping a hole would open up and swallow him if his Dad did actually start dancing. Or, better still, swallow his dad.

27 A MOST WICKED DEAD

The projector fired up. George's dad flicked out his leg like a seasoned street mover. But there was no music. Projected behind the stage, was a video of the prop room at the other end of the hall. The audience looked at one another, murmurs rising. It made no sense. George's dad dropped his moves, turning to see what was going on.

"What's this...?" said Mrs T marched back to the projector. Pickled Daniels came into view on the video.

"This is it," Marley whispered to George excitedly. "This is the video. This is brilliant."

Pickled Daniels had been busy minding her own business. She had one of her terrible headaches and nausea from hearing so much laughter, it was starting to take its toll. Nothing had worked, nothing. Every trap, plan and trick had failed this evening. Everyone in her darling school, and everyone happy. Horrible.

The video took her by surprise, she wasn't

sure what it was. She scowled at the screen.

The whole audience was silent. Mrs T was hypnotised, not really sure what to do. Then the entire dreadful episode played out. They saw Pickled Daniels drifting around picking up costumes and depositing them into her bag, tearing out pages from scripts and defacing props. And the most wicked deed of all, deliberately forcing George's magic box off the table, smashing it into tiny pieces. The audience gasped before the video cut off and the room was plunged into darkness again.

Pickled Daniels quivered, her face turned from grey to white. *Where did the video come from? Should she run? Should she hide?* She couldn't! All eyes in the room had turned towards her.

Eventually, the silence was broken by Mrs T. "Lights please," she said sternly. The lights came up, and Mrs T's face was contorted in anger. Forcibly hauling Pickled Daniels onto the stage, her rage seethed. Mrs T's mouth had stopped working, her bottom lip quivering in a fury. They stood to face each other. Pickled Daniels appeared old and lost, tears gathering in her eyes.

Finally, Mrs T spoke. "Never in all my time as a teacher have I seen such a wicked or contemptible act, Mrs Daniels. Your actions are inexcusable and intolerable. The children and teachers have worked for weeks on this show, and this is how you treat them? You will stand here right now and explain yourself. I expect a full apology." She crossed her arms and glared at Pickled Daniels. The room was mute, waiting for the confession to come.

George and Marley stared at each other in disbelief. At last, their efforts had paid off. This is what they had wanted.

"Erm...well I was..." Pickled Daniels mumbled. This was turning out to be a very tough day.

There was a dreadful commotion at the back of the hall. Everyone turned to see what was going on.

"Stop right there," boomed a loud voice. Firefighter O'Gorman strode into view, accompanied by two junior firefighters. The audience wasn't sure now if this was all an act for the finale or real life.

"Firefighter O'Gorman, what is it?" asked Mrs T, a frown on her brow.

"It's like this Margaret," bellowed O'Gorman joining her on stage. He didn't know how to talk normally, and the stage had given him some additional self-confidence. "I've come to talk to

Mrs Daniels. You see following our investigation we now know that your school fire was started deliberately, and we think Mrs Daniels did it...We want our award back." He stared at Pickled Daniels with disgust. Mrs T's rage soared to new levels.

"Now what have you got to say for yourself?" Mrs T demanded. O'Gorman towered over them with his hands on his hips. Pickled Daniels was mulling it over, *should she come clean or try to get away with it?* The audience held their breath.

George's mum was enjoying the evening enormously, this was better than any soap opera on the TV. She delved into her sweet bag for another chocolate, waiting for the action to continue.

"You see Mrs Tinsley," Pickled Daniels started timidly. "I'm sick of everyone being in my school all hours of the day. It don't seem fair. This is my school. I've been working here for years. I look after it and everyone takes advantage. You're all are so happy to be here. It was me who turned the tea purple, blocked the toilets, put stinking cheese under the stage and released me spiders. I started the fire by mistake, I dropped me candle. I was only trying to start the smoke alarm. I was just trying to get everyone to go home." Pickled Daniels was close to tears. Mrs T's face was purple with rage, her eyes glittering with fury.

"What a load of twaddle. What you did was bullying and inexcusable vile behaviour and I won't have it in my school. And to start a fire and pretend you had actually put it out is well...well...it's criminal. I'm afraid Mrs Daniels that you are fired. Your services are no longer required in our school. We are a community, and together we are better. I can't have one person defacing the school and spoiling it for everyone else." The room erupted into applause.

Pickled Daniels stared at the floor. O'Gorman stepped forward. "You are going to have to come with me now Mrs Daniels, we need to get to the bottom of this fire. We have some questions for you." O'Gorman signalled for the firefighters to move in. Abruptly another voice came out from the audience.

"Agnes?"

The room went quiet, everyone turned to see who had shouted.

"Agnes, is that you?" croaked an old voice from the second row. Pickled Daniels turned to peer at the audience. She recognised him immediately. Her face changed to one of utter astonishment.

"Ernie?" Pickled Daniels replied trying to get the person into focus. Everyone turned to look at Great Uncle Ernie. Ernie rose and pushed past Sam and Mrs Ferris, making his way to the stage.

"Agnes it is you! After all these years..." Ernie's eyes filled with tears. Pickled Daniels inched slowly forward. Ernie raised his hands to meet hers.

"Agnes, I thought I'd never see you again. Why didn't you write?" Uncle Ernie was tripping over his words. George's dad came to the front and helped him up to the stage. Ernie and Pickled Daniels embraced.

"Ernie. I couldn't you see," Pickled Daniels replied, tears streaming down her cheeks. "Me father thought you were no good for me. He wouldn't let me. When I did write you'd moved on, I couldn't find you. But I've thought about you Ernie, all the time. I've still got this photo of you." Pickled Daniels extracted the creased, beaten photograph out of her pocket holding it out to him. "It's all I had left in my life, this one photo of you and my painting of Fifi, the dog. After all, it was you saved her Ernie when we first met" Teenagers in the audience extracted their mobiles to video the encounter.

"This is my sweetheart, Agnes, who I told you about, I haven't seen her for over sixty years," Uncle Ernie explained. "She's not got a rotten bone in her body."

"Well, clearly she has, did you not just see what she did." Mrs T stepped in to take control of the bizarre situation. "I'm sorry to break up your happy reunion, but Mrs Daniels does have some explaining to do so your little reconciliation will have to wait."

Mrs T signalled for the firefighters to come forward. O'Gorman had a look of utter distaste on his face, his arms folded squarely, looking ready for a fire if it should spring up anytime soon.

"I'm coming with you Agnes, you're not in this alone. Now I've found you again I'm not letting you go," said Uncle Ernie holding onto Pickled Daniels, gazing lovingly at her.

"Ernie. All this time I've been thinking about you. About the things we could have done, the family we could have had. It keeps me awake at night Ernie. It really does. Why didn't you find me? My life could have been so different. I've missed you Ernie." She planted her filthy arms around Ernie, sobbing into his shoulder. Pickled Daniels turned towards Mrs Tinsley with tears in her eyes, the audience clearly enjoying the melodrama.

"I'm sorry Mrs Tinsley." Pickled Daniels blubbed, her eyes full of tears.

"It's not me you need to apologise to, is it? It's all the children who have had their hopes and dreams destroyed with your nasty plans. You need to apologise to them all."

But before Pickled Daniels could respond she was marched off. The audience watched the procession as O'Gorman, and the firefighters led Pickled Daniels and Ernie out of the school.

The incident had finished the show. No finale would top what the audience had just witnessed.

George and Marley had been quiet during the whole episode. Now they both beamed. George's dad came to the back of the stage to speak to them.

"How did this get on my phone, did you take it without my permission?" he asked looking at them intently, his face darkening.

"Sorry Dad, we didn't want to take your phone but it was important. We wanted to get evidence about Pickled Daniels. It was Sam's idea. She told us to use your phone to record the proof," explained George trying to pass the buck.

"It's OK," replied Dad softly, ruffling his hair. "You both did really well. I always thought there was something odd about her. I'm just disappointed that I haven't had a chance to perform my dance. Perhaps there's still time?" He pushed his arm into the air ready to start the dance move.

"Dad.....nooooooooooooo oooo..." George screamed.

Mrs Tinsley signalled for the audience to quieten down.

"I will not have our whole evening ruined by that woman. We have one final announcement to make. The prize for the best act will now be presented." Mrs Walker gripped a small silver cup and a gigantic sack of sweets.

"Thank you, Mrs Tinsley. It has been a hard decision on who to award the top prize to, but we feel we've come up with a clear winner. This particular pupil has worked very hard on their act and clearly loves what they do. The judges felt they had mastered all the main elements of their performance and it was almost faultless."

George looked at Marley, braced for his name to be read out. He brushed the front of his costume to make sure he looked presentable, ready to collect the prize.

"And the winner is..." Mrs Walker exaggerated her pause to give the announcement extra tension. George felt like he was about to burst waiting for his name to be read out.

"...Phoebe Ferris!"

Phoebe pranced around in her green tutu to rapturous applause. Marley poked George in the ribs laughing. George was shocked and devastated. To lose the coveted prize is one thing, to lose to your little sister dancing in a sickening tutu is altogether worse. Mrs Walker handed the cup and sweets to Phoebe, shaking her hand vigorously in the process.

"Well done Phoebe, you gave a wonderful performance."

"Thank you, Mrs Tinsley." Phoebe discreetly stuck her tongue out at George before she turned to the audience and gave a little curtsy. Mum and Sam clapped enthusiastically from the second row.

The show was over. As the audience clapped the children filed from the set leaving Phoebe stood by herself soaking up the glory until eventually, the stage went dark.

Children filed back, dressed and ready to go home with their parents. George and Marley came straight out to meet Mum, Dad and Sam. The audience was dispersing, chattering about Pickled Daniels and her bizarre behaviour.

"Who'd have believed it ay? Great Uncle Ernie and Mrs Daniels knowing each. I suppose I need to go to the fire station to find Ernie. So, what have you lot been up to then over the last few weeks? How did you get that video?" Dad asked.

"That was me." Sam smiled. "I helped them. But they did all the planning and hard work." She looked at Marley and gave him a wink. Marley's cheeks shone red. George beamed with pride over the whole episode.

"Well done to the three of you," Dad replied.

"Why was she so horrible mum? Most people love our school." George asked, looking puzzled.

"She's obviously had a very sad life. Sometimes people do the most dreadful things when bad things have happened to them. It's sometimes easy to lose sight of what is right and wrong. I'm sure they'll make sure she gets the help she needs. You don't need to worry about your school. Everyone does love it," said Mum smiling at George.

"Well, she certainly was a nasty piece of work. I don't suppose we'll be seeing any more of her for a while," added Dad.

"We might do..." George's mum gave them a strange smile. "...If Ernie marries her!"

George. The World's First Baking Magician

ACKNOWLEDGEMENTS

I'd like to thank Embla Granqvist for her magnificent illustrations. Robin for his cool cover. Hannah Sheppard for her guidance through the writing process. To my beautiful family for their patience and support. Finally, to Julien Smith, the author of "The Flinch" - who I've never met, but who made me write this.

Printed in Great Britain
by Amazon